D1095721

Beverly Hills Prep

ROYALTY

SHANNON LAYNE

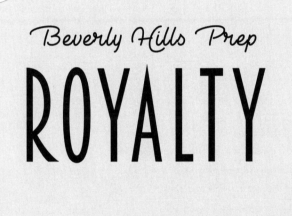

EPIC Escape

An Imprint of EPIC Press
abdopublishing.com

Royalty
Beverly Hills Prep: Book #6

abdopublishing.com

Published by EPIC Press, a division of ABDO, PO Box 398166, Minneapolis, Minnesota 55439. Copyright © 2019 by Abdo Consulting Group, Inc. International copyrights reserved in all countries. No part of this book may be reproduced in any form without written permission from the publisher. Escape™ is a trademark and logo of EPIC Press.

Printed in the United States of America, North Mankato, Minnesota.
052018
092018

Cover design by Laura Mitchell
Edited by Ryan Hume

Library of Congress Cataloging-in-Publication Data

Library of Congress Control Number: 2016962593

Publisher's Cataloging in Publication Data

Names: Layne, Shannon, author.
Title: Royalty/ by Shannon Layne
Description: Minneapolis, MN : EPIC Press, 2019 | Series: Beverly hills prep; #6
Summary: Ophelia has been expelled from boarding schools and prep schools all over the world, and her wealthy grandmother had to pull some major strings to get her accepted to Beverly Hills Prep. She tries to keep her head down and focus on her art, but it's not always easy. Ophelia hopes she can stick to the straight and narrow at Beverly Hills Prep, but her rebelliousness might land her in major trouble—for the last time.
Identifiers: ISBN 9781680767131 (lib. bdg.) | ISBN 9781680767698 (ebook)
Subjects: LCSH: Teenage girls--Conduct of life--Fiction. | Expulsion of students--Fiction. | Private preparatory schools--Fiction. | Teenage girls--Fiction | Young adult fiction.
Classification: DDC [FIC]--dc23

For the girls who are rebels at heart.

*There are some who can live without wild things
and some who cannot.*

—Aldo Leopold

Chapter One

Her new roommate's name was Darlene. That was all Ophelia knew about her; that, and that she was British. That much had been made clear in the first three seconds that they'd spoken while Ophelia was moving her stuff into her new bedroom.

"Just don't make a mess, please. I'm not telling you what to do, or anything, but I prefer this space to be clean and tidy." Darlene blinked rapidly as she scuttled around, her eyes enormous behind the kind of huge glasses Ophelia had been sure only existed in cartoons.

Oh man, she sounds like a nut job.

Ophelia physically bit her tongue, trying to stay calm. There was no reason to bite this girl's head off; she was an idiot, but that wasn't enough of a reason. At least, that was what Ophelia's therapist would've said in this situation. She'd been seeing him all year, ever since she got into Beverly Hills Prep in the fall. It was part of the agreement arranged with the headmistress; Ophelia was on academic probation for an entire year, with required biweekly counseling sessions, and drug tests. The drug tests bothered her the most, but the school had insisted on it. She supposed it wasn't fair for her to bristle at being treated like a criminal when it seemed she'd practically spent more time fighting to stay out of juvenile hall than to stay in school, sometimes.

"I'm not going to mess anything up," said Ophelia to Darlene. "Please just leave me alone." The last of her boxes had arrived in her new room and all she wanted was to unpack in peace, without this girl leaning over her shoulder.

"There's still a lot of stuff in the living room, actually."

"I'll get to it," said Ophelia through gritted teeth.

"Okay. I just have a very particular system in place. I'm going to be valedictorian of our class, and to do that I need to have everything exactly as I need it or I can't study."

Ophelia's head was starting to hurt. She brushed back a lock of glossy black hair that had slid over her shoulder and straightened up, turning to face Darlene.

"I'm not hard to live with," she said quietly. "My personal living habits will include staying far, far away from you, I can pretty much guarantee that."

"Oh, okay."

"What? Are you offended now? You basically just told me that I need to tiptoe around you at all times. I said that I would do my best to leave you alone, because that's all I want, too. What more do you want from me?"

"Nothing, I guess. I didn't mean that we couldn't be friends, you know."

Now her tone was wheedling, like she wanted something from Ophclia. Now that Darlene had gotten her to agree to be a good roommate, it sounded like she wanted to play nice.

"I don't want to be friends," Ophelia said. "I want to coexist peacefully with you. Like Belgium and Sweden."

"Uh huh," said Darlene. Ophelia frowned as she realized Darlene was starting to take interest in Ophelia's boxes, craning her neck to see into the bedroom.

"The girl who used to live with me had a nervous breakdown," said Darlene matter-of-factly, now studying her gnawed fingernails. "Everyone says that she couldn't handle the pressure of being in a school like this."

"I'm sorry to hear that, I guess." What else was she supposed to say?

"There's a lot they say about you, too, you know."

Again, Ophelia fought back a flash of temper. This girl was going to make her insane. Now that she'd started talking, it seemed like she couldn't stop.

"I don't care what anyone says about me."

"Is it true that you're related to a princess? And that your mother wouldn't take your father's last name?"

That did it.

Ophelia whirled around, a shoulder knocking into her solid wood dresser as she faced Darlene and scowled.

"Keep your mouth shut about me, and about my family," she hissed. "I don't care that you're my roommate now, okay? If I hear you running your mouth about me, you will regret it."

"Okay, okay." Darlene backed out of Ophelia's room slowly, her hands up as though Ophelia was pointing a gun at her. "No problem, Ophelia. Calm down."

"Just call me Lia."

Darlene wasn't her friend, but the name Ophelia didn't fit her. It never had.

When Darlene finally retreated back into the common room, Ophelia shut and locked her bedroom door. She leaned her forehead against the door and sighed, rubbing a hand over her temples. Of course she'd gotten stuck with the roommate who insisted upon total cleanliness and then wouldn't stop talking in an accent that sometimes made it hard for Ophelia to even understand what she was saying. Ophelia sat down on one of her moving boxes, rubbing her temples. She missed Margot, and that was strange for her. It was unusual for Ophelia to miss anyone. But she did; she missed Margot's loud laugh and the way she made Ophelia feel completely comfortable without doing anything. There weren't a lot of people who could do that for her, and now she had to start over again. That much, at least, she was used to.

Ophelia had been to somewhere around six schools in the past three years. No place seemed to stick—she'd gotten in trouble for typical things, like fighting or smarting off to one too many teachers, but there had been other incidents. There was that time that a fire mysteriously started in her room, and the time that one of the girls who'd been teasing her woke up with her entire ponytail cut off. These were incidents that could never be definitively pinned on Ophelia, but the rumors started, anyway, and it was never long before everything was blamed on her.

By the time she was starting at her third school there was no point in trying to pretend to act like a good little girl anyway, because no one would believe her no matter what she said. What was the point in denying it? It was always her fault, and she had run out of excuses a long time ago. She just sat there sullenly during disciplinary meetings, when before she used to rail and scream and make a scene. Sometimes she still did that, just for kicks, but more often she looked at her nails, bored, waiting for the meeting to end.

The third school had barely lasted a week and a half before they expelled her; then, there was the school that no one got kicked out of. It was buried in the depths of the English countryside with nothing but moor and grass and wilderness on all sides. To get into town there was only the train and that took nearly half a day. It was the loneliest place that Lia had ever been, but it was peaceful. She was even a little sad when two months later she got on the train with her bags to leave again. That had been one of the worst times—she'd gotten into a fight with another girl who was also studying abroad, a brunette with a permanent sneer plastered across her freckled face. That incident in itself hadn't been the terrible part, although one of her fingernails had scratched Ophelia right at her hairline and left a pale white scar that had never been completely erased. The worst part had been the security team that met her at the train station and took her away for the first time. Her family name had kept her out of the worst situations, and Lia had to be thankful for that, but that time not even her grandmother could save her.

The sound of Darlene shuffling into place on the couch and her computer turning on snapped Lia out of the memory. She stood up, sighing, nudging one of the boxes over with her foot. She'd been at this school since fall, at least, and had managed to not get kicked out yet. It was nearly spring, and school would be out in just a few months.

Just a little while longer, Ophelia thought to herself as she dug out pajamas. *Just a little longer, and then it will be summer and I can spend it in Rome or Paris or wherever I want with Grandmamma, just visiting museums and art galleries.* Sometimes it seemed like summer would never get here. Lia grabbed her head-phones from her bag and lay down on her bed. The bed, at least, was made since it came with the suite. They'd given her several options for sheet colors, and even the bedspread, but Lia didn't care at this point. It was ironic, because most of her life was spent considering aesthetics and color palettes and how to translate everything she felt inside to paper or to canvas, but when it came to her room all she wanted was dark colors. Gray was her favorite. It reminded her of the sky in England, and cloudy days were always calming to her. Usually she chose reds and oranges and deep colors when she was painting or drawing, but that wasn't what she wanted in her bedroom. Lia chose a punk rock music station, sliding her earphones over her head. Then, she let everything else dissolve as she closed her eyes.

Chapter Two

Lia woke up the next morning with her laptop still playing music through her headphones, but she'd slipped them off her head sometime in the night so she could only faintly hear The Ramones playing now. She rubbed her eyes, sitting up from where she'd fallen asleep in a nest of silk pillows and the white Egyptian cotton sheets. Beverly Hills Prep didn't skimp when it came to the amenities—that was one thing she couldn't complain about.

The sun was barely coming through the blinds, so it couldn't be time for class yet. Checking the Apple watch that her dad had gotten her for her last birthday, Ophelia confirmed that it was barely six in the morning. She would've preferred to lie back down and sleep until noon, but in her months at Beverly Hills Prep she'd forced herself to get used to actually showing up for her classes. After she'd been called in to see the headmistress barely a week into the school year for skipping, Ophelia had gritted her teeth and resigned herself to toeing the line. Of all the school administrators she'd scoffed at over the years, Headmistress Chambers was not someone to be messed with. And Ophelia didn't want to end up in juvenile detention again. There were a lot of punishments that she'd been subjected to when she'd started getting into trouble at school, but that was the only one she was truly terrified of repeating. She'd never admit it to anyone, not even her therapist, but she felt a deep dread at the thought of repeating that experience.

Speaking of her therapist, she had an appointment with him today after school. While she'd grown to grudgingly trust him over the course of the year, Lia still had a hard time opening herself up to his questions. But progress had been made, certainly, since the beginning. As she stepped into the shower, Lia's mind drifted back to the first steps she'd taken inside the hallowed *freaking* halls of Beverly Hills Prep.

When Lia had walked through the doors of Beverly Hills Prep as a third-year transfer in the fall, she'd hated the place on sight. That wasn't unusual for her at all, but this time it was more personal. Lia had walked over the marble floor of the foyer, listening to the sound of her footsteps reverberating in the great hall as her driver had tugged her luggage behind her.

"Your suite is ready," the headmistress had said ahead of her, turning to face Lia with a swish of her robes. "You should still have your initiation packet with the information regarding school policies and regulations. Study Hall will be held tonight beginning at six-thirty p.m. sharp. Dinner will be held from four-thirty p.m. until six p.m. Do you have any questions?"

"No," said Lia shortly. She scowled as one of her bags tipped from the tower of luggage and landed on the floor with a clack.

"Tomorrow morning will be the first day of classes. You'll find a few sets of the school uniform in your closet already. Any extra sets you may need can be purchased from the school uniform facility."

Lia had seen the uniforms. She'd had to wear one at every other school she'd ever attended, so it wasn't that big a deal. There were always ways to get around the strict regulations, but she did admit that the ones at Beverly Hills Prep were some of the most stringent she'd ever seen, all the way down to the socks or tights. But that just made it more of a challenge.

"Your nail polish and makeup will have to go," the headmistress continued.

Lia snorted, and rolled her eyes.

"Is there a problem, Ms. Koroleva?"

"Do I really need to take my nail polish off?"

The headmistress just lowered her gaze to Ophelia's moody, plum-colored nails and then back up to look her squarely in the eyes.

"Yes," she said simply. "And light makeup is allowed for the seniors, but not third years."

"Whatever," Lia said, rolling her eyes.

"I really advise you not to start here with an attitude, Ms. Koroleva."

"Look, I don't need your advice, okay? I'm just here to spend my two years and graduate, and then I'm gone."

"The conditions for your attendance here are not lax, Ms. Koroleva. You truly can't afford any slipups. Two years is a short period of time relatively speaking, but for a teenager it's much longer than you'd think."

"Again, thanks a lot for stating the obvious."

The headmistress narrowed her eyes and Ophelia glared right back. She wasn't afraid of this old woman, no matter how much she managed to seem as though she were simply towering over Ophelia with a look that could cut ice. Almost against her will, Ophelia squirmed uncomfortably. Someone had to break the silence.

"Sorry," she muttered.

"Your first appointment with your therapist will be tomorrow afternoon. We'll outline the schedule for the rest of your tests and such after that. You'll also be expected to maintain at least a 3.0 grade point average."

"Wait, what? Why?"

"That's part of the agreement, Ophelia."

"Don't call me that," snapped Lia.

"What do you prefer to be called?"

"Lia. Just Lia."

"Alright—*Lia*, then. I apologize. I wasn't aware of your preference."

Lia slowly unclenched the fists that she'd unconsciously clenched when the headmistress had called her Ophelia. Her grandmother was the only person whom she let call her that.

"So, why the grade point average rule?" asked Lia. The headmistress had sighed.

"Let's go into my office and talk about this. Your bags will be taken to your suite in the meantime."

The headmistress had walked Lia down the hallway toward her office, leaving Lia plenty of time to get a good look at the place that would be her home for the next two years. It was certainly impressive, with great sweeping staircases and dark burnished wood everywhere, but to Lia it looked a lot like every other prison that she'd been locked up in for the past two years. She was raised in a home holding relics from the Romanov dynasty, and it was the coldest place in the world. Just because a place was beautiful and lavishly furnished didn't mean it was a good place; you could still feel trapped in houses with vaulted ceilings and enormous crystal chandeliers, and windows that no one ever opened. She should know.

Lia stepped out of the shower and dried her long, dark hair with a towel. Her eyes in the mirror were the color of a thunderstorm, gray and fierce, identical to her mother's. Sighing, Ophelia dressed in her uniform and put on a blazer. Grabbing her nail polish, Lia carefully painted her thumbnail a blinding shade of hot pink. By painting one nail a day and changing the nail and the color constantly, she was always evading teacher orders to take her nail polish off. It was a minor offense, but Lia enjoyed it. Between the daily nail polish changes, and her tendency to wear long socks with designs that were just barely outside the dress code, Lia made the teachers a little insane. And in doing so, she kept herself sane for another day.

Chapter Three

Another major difference in Lia's life since attending Beverly Hills Prep was the fact that she actually went to all of her classes, and not just the ones she was interested in. At her other schools, she'd had no desire whatsoever to sit in classrooms where the teacher was going to drone on and on about American history or English literature or, God forbid, any sort of math. Most of the time she skipped any of those classes she possibly could, and holed herself up for hours on end in dark rooms, studios, and the occasional pottery room. If she could take an entire course load of nothing but art classes, then she'd be there early every single day—but as her teachers kept reminding her, that wasn't how high school worked. Passing math and science and everything else was necessary to get into any of the art colleges that she had her eye on, and since Beverly Hills Prep, Lia found herself actually checking off requirements from the list of core class prerequisites. It was almost like she'd given up on the idea of getting into a college of the arts at all until she was forced to pass the classes that she needed to get there. And while her grades in math, science, and literature were all passing, nothing special, her passion still lay in her art classes.

Since she was little she'd spent all the extra time she could find drawing, painting, or basically creating anything she could. As a preschooler, all that really meant was that she'd been really into finger painting, but as she got older, it had become a passion. And she was good at it—so good that her art teachers had told her to look into schools like the Rhode Island School of Design or the San Francisco Art Institute. But she'd always been kicked out of schools before anything stuck. Next year she'd start applying to universities, and for the first time Lia was concerned about things like her grades and her portfolio. This year would be the year she'd submit pieces for the Advanced Placement tests and there was also a major showcase at the end of the year where students were able to actually display pieces for other students, parents, faculty, and guests—guests like the deans of admission for more than twenty different art schools around the country. Lia had been preparing all year, and she still hadn't chosen the piece she wanted to display. She had a few that were still in the creation process, and a couple finished ones, but nothing that really tugged at her. There was the watercolor painting she'd done in the fall, and the charcoal self-portraits, but nothing was special enough. There was only one spot for her work since she was only a third year, and the one piece that she chose would be the only one that the scouts and admissions professionals saw. It had to be perfect.

Lia was still thinking about her art presentation

when she left her bedroom with her bag slung over her shoulder and headed to breakfast. Darlene's room was empty. Lia was pretty sure that she'd been awake since before dawn to study or something. The girl was insane. Yawning, Lia locked their suite behind her and headed to the dining hall. She needed buckets and buckets of coffee if she was going to make it through this day.

Lia inhaled as she entered the dining hall; it smelled like cinnamon and coffee and vanilla and she was starving. Even though it seemed like half of the girls here subsisted on grapefruit and oxygen, one of Lia's favorite parts of every day was when she got to eat. She loaded her tray with handmade Swedish twisted cinnamon rolls, a still-hot cherry Danish, two handfuls of strawberries, a chocolate-chip Belgian waffle with a splatter of hand-whipped cream, and an enormous latte from the beverage cart. Balancing her tray, Lia scanned the room and then walked to an empty table. She used to eat with Margot, whose fiery hair she could see a few tables over, but that didn't seem like such a good idea anymore. But that didn't mean it wasn't hard. Margot had been her first friend at Beverly Hills Prep. She was the opposite of all the other girls that Lia had come across in her time at boarding schools across the country. Margot was warm and friendly, and she had a killer sense of humor, and she didn't seem to care when Lia messed up the common room with her paintings or drawings. She'd even given Ophelia a new nickname—Fi, that no one had ever called her before. Lia didn't really have friends at any of her other schools. Girls tended to stay away from her, and whisper about her, and that was fine with Lia most of the time. It was more her reputation than anything else that kept people away. But Margot had been different; Margot wasn't afraid of her, and something about her had been disarming to Lia's normally prickly exterior.

Lia finished her Belgian waffle right as the bells began to ring, signaling the start of her first class. She sighed and carried her tray dutifully to the trash can, grabbed her backpack, and headed to her

Environmental Science class. All she had to do was make it through the morning; the second half of her day was pretty much exclusively art. She was enrolled in an awesome photography class, level three drawing and composition, and a watercolor and charcoal-specific elective that she'd somehow managed to squeeze into her schedule. Lia walked into her Environmental Science class and pulled out her book. In her head, she was already trying to come up with a new idea for the end of the year exhibition.

Chapter Four

Lia squeaked by with a "B" on her Environmental Science quiz, and she'd remembered that her teacher for Algebra II had hinted at a pop quiz, so she'd studied ahead of time and didn't think she'd done too badly on that one, either. For so long she'd failed nearly every quiz and test she'd taken, that it still felt novel just to pass. Her mother had hated how Lia refused to put forward any effort at all in class, and that was at least half of the reason that she never did. There weren't a lot of ways to make her parents mad, but Lia made sure to hit on all the possibilities. It was seeing her mom upset that made life worth living.

Lia wolfed down an entire ham sandwich at lunch and headed straight to her photography classroom. The teacher nodded at her as she walked in. Even though class didn't start for another fifteen minutes, Lia liked to come early, before all the other students showed up to annoy her. She went straight into the darkroom, letting her eyes adjust to the dark and eerie red lighting, and then went to the developing station. There were a few of her prints that were still drying—a still life and a few that she'd taken of the architecture on campus. Lia's taste in photography leaned toward simple, clean lines, and crisp compositions. Beverly Hills Prep offered no shortage of photography opportunities. The place was like Hogwarts, but instead of magical creatures, within the walls lived annoying girls. *What a trade-off.*

The spinning door of the darkroom turned as someone else came in. Lia frowned, but continued to focus on the print that was going through the developing process in the first tray.

"So," said a voice, "I see you moved out of Margot's room."

Lia knew the voice. The girl it belonged to had been harassing her all year for reasons that, to Lia, were still unclear. It was like she just enjoyed seeing Lia fight to stay calm. Come to think of it, that was probably the entire reason. The girl was sadistic.

"What do you care, Grace?" said Lia. She was beyond tired of this harassment. Grace didn't scare her, but that didn't mean Lia didn't find her annoying. And after months of dealing with this, Lia's already low patience was reaching desperate points.

"I just find it interesting."

Lia raised her eyebrows, meeting Grace's eyes for the first time. Grace stood with her arms crossed, her weight on one hip. Her face held the half-smirk, half-sneer that Lia had become annoyingly familiar with over the past year.

"Get out of my way," said Lia, moving to the second tray.

"I just wanted to make sure that you weren't going

to go into any detail about why you decided to switch rooms."

"I'm a terrible snorer, actually," said Lia. "Margot couldn't stand it, poor girl, so I decided to spare her."

Grace scowled; she had the sense of humor of an ox.

"Keep your mouth shut, Ophelia," said Grace, and Lia didn't correct the use of her full name.

Lia snorted out a laugh and moved to the third developing tray, letting her print fully submerge and then flipping it with the plastic tongs. A girl like Grace threatening Lia was like a mouse threatening a lion. She could squeak all she wanted, even bite if she felt like it, but if it ever came to a real fight there was no doubt who would emerge victorious. Lia might have been forced to walk on eggshells in some aspects of her attendance at Beverly Hills Prep, but her family and Grace's were on completely different levels. There was no need for Lia to walk on eggshells with her, although she did have to refrain from physically punching her the way she'd really, really wanted.

Grace was a nobody. Lia, regardless of the rules she was forced to abide by at Beverly Hills Prep, would never be a nobody. Maybe it wasn't fair, maybe it wasn't politically correct, but those were the facts. And Lia knew that much of the reason that Grace was so antagonistic toward her was because she knew that she could be as mean to Lia as she could possibly be, and it wouldn't change anything in the real world.

"I mean it," said Grace, following Lia as she moved to the last tray. "I'm not joking around here. I know that you know certain things because you lived in that room with her."

"Whatever, Grace," sighed Lia. "This conversation is boring me. I think you should go."

Grace's face appeared mottled, even in the dim lighting of the dark room.

"You might think you're the queen of the world," hissed Grace, "but you aren't. Not in here. I don't care who your family is. I call the shots in this school, so you should start treating me with some respect."

"You sound asinine," said Lia, fighting against the

vicious flare of temper. *Visualize an open sea,* her psychologist would say. *A wide, blue, calm ocean.* "And there's nothing you can say that's going to make me respect you. You're just a big bully, and you've got Margot mixed up in something that I can assure you I want no part of."

"How do I know that you won't say anything, huh? Everyone else in this place listens to me. I can trust that no one is going to rat me out—but you always refuse to cooperate."

"Get out of my face, Grace," said Lia quietly. She turned to face Grace, finally, her patience completely gone. "I mean it. Just go, now, because I cannot listen to you for another second and you aren't worth the trouble I'm in if I sock you right now."

"You wouldn't dare," hissed Grace.

"Just go. Trust me. You don't want to push me on this."

There was a moment of tense silence, and then Grace turned and angrily pushed through the spinning darkroom door. Lia unclenched her fists very slowly. Maybe it was a good thing that she had that appointment with her psychologist today. She could tell him how she managed to go another day without engaging in physical violence. The good doctor would be so proud.

Chapter Five

As the bell finally rang and signaled the end of her last class, Lia sighed and moved out of her seat with a combination of resignation and relief. Her classes were finished, at least, but now she had to meet Dr. Lowenstein. Their sessions ran a lot more smoothly now than they had when they'd first met, but Lia still had a hard time handling someone prying into her personal life day after day. Dr. Lowenstein had explained to her patiently that he wasn't prying, that he was a licensed professional trying to help Lia work through some complex emotional baggage and *blah blah blah*, but that only helped about half the time. Still, progress was progress, and Lia had grown to like Lowenstein as the year went on.

Lia walked out of the classroom and down the hallway, trying to avoid the sea of girls walking by her in groups, gossiping about whose skirt was the shortest and who was headed back to the surgeon after a botched nose job. A few glanced at Lia, but their gazes skittered quickly away. Lia figured that there were some girls who had heard about her reputation and were afraid that she'd literally punch them in the face, and there were some who were more interested in the rumors about her family than asking her about them to her face.

She might have been able to talk about her family, at least a little, if someone would just ask her in a nice way. But no one was brave enough to do that. Even Margot had stayed away from that subject. Lia understood—her family name was intimidating, but still. She was a normal person. She hadn't asked to be born into a family that was descended from Russian royalty. In her entire life she'd never even been to Russia, which seemed crazy considering the time she'd spent abroad. But she'd never been *there*. Grandmamma didn't want to take her until she was older, and there was no one else she wanted to go with.

Lia followed the south side of campus, walking along the edge of the arboretum until she reached the administrative building. The air was still crisp and cool, but the sun was shining strongly and Lia could feel the warmth seeping through her stupid blazer. It felt nice; it felt like spring. Lia pushed open the double doors of the administrative building and walked down the hardwood floors, her Mary Janes clicking gently on the floor.

"Those shoes have too high of a heel, Ms. Koroleva," said a teacher reproachfully as she passed. Lia smiled and nodded, and continued walking.

"I'll make a note of that, Mrs. Schneider."

"Cheeky little thing," muttered Mrs. Schneider, with her tightly pursed lips. Lia ignored her breezily, and instead knocked briskly on the door of the medical wing. It stung a little, knowing that she had to go into the medical wing for her sessions. It made her feel like a loon, but that was where the psychologist's office was, so she had no choice. Lia sidled through the open space, past the nurse's station, and let herself quietly into the small room adjacent to the east side of the building. It wasn't a large space, but the sun shone through the big window and there were just two chairs and thankfully no couch to make her feel like an invalid. Waiting for Lia was a man who was already sitting in one of the big leather chairs. He had large glasses and a large nose, and a salt-and-pepper beard with dark hair that was graying on the edges. He stood barely taller than Lia herself—all in all, he was a completely genial-looking, unassuming man, and Lia appreciated nothing more than his approachability, so different from herself.

"What's up, Lowenstein?" said Lia, tossing her blazer onto the seat of the other chair.

"Good afternoon, Lia. Would you like something to drink? Iced tea?"

"I'll take water with lemon if you've got it."

"Coming right up."

The doctor heaved himself out of the chair and over to the mini fridge. With his bowed legs and his slightly stooped shoulders, though he couldn't have been more than in his mid-fifties, he was the least intimidating person Lia had ever met. He didn't find Lia intimidating, either, like so many other adults did. Lia had learned that on their very first meeting.

The first time Lia had set foot in this very office, she'd only been a student at Beverly Hills Prep for about thirty-six hours. Seeing a psychologist was part of the agreement that she'd signed, and so seeing Dr. Lowenstein was contingent in Lia staying at Beverly Hills Prep. She knew that, but that didn't mean she felt like taking it easy on him. When the doctor walked in right on the dot at three-twenty p.m., the time of their appointment, Lia was already waiting, sitting in what was clearly the doctor's chair.

"Hello, Ophelia," Dr. Lowenstein had said, his briefcase carried in one hand.

Lia hadn't answered.

The doctor had walked across the room to the other chair and sat down, opening his briefcase on his lap. There was an open desk in the corner that he could've utilized, but that was behind the chair that Lia was occupying, so he was forced to balance her file on his knobby knees. Lia had scrutinized him carefully, noting the horrible brown sweater vest, the kind eyes.

"Perhaps we should get started," said the doctor. "My name is Dr. Lowenstein. Why don't you start by telling me something about yourself?"

Lia had glared, a withering stare cutting through narrowed eyes. There was silence.

The doctor had flipped open Lia's file, an enormous envelope stuffed to the brim with papers and slips. Lia had eyed it with hatred. Her file seemed to follow her everywhere she went, a constant reminder of all the ways she'd ever messed up. No matter what school she transferred to, her file followed, like an evil shadow.

"There's quite a lot of information in here," said the doctor. "I've spent some time going through it all."

More silence from Lia.

"It seems like you have major issues dealing with authority, Ophelia."

"You picked right up on that," said Lia, her first words of the session.

"So you acknowledge the problem."

"I guess."

The doctor had blinked at Lia, and the seconds ticked off on the clock on the wall. Lia settled into her chair, crossing her legs comfortably.

"So, we're going to meet twice every week for at least the remainder of this year," the doctor tried again. "I'd really like to get to know you. Whenever you're ready to start talking, about anything, anything at all—I'm here to listen."

Lia had smirked at him, settling deeper into her

chair. Over the years she'd been subjected to every kind of psychologist imaginable. There were the ones who tried to wheedle her into talking, the ones that were stern with her, and the ones who tried to make her laugh. They'd all failed, one after the other—Lia counted one particular victory in which the poor woman had quit after only two sessions. None of the professionals hired by schools or her parents had succeeded in pulling anything out of Lia besides sullen silences, sarcasm, and the occasional angry outburst. Why should this man be any different?

They spent the rest of the hour that first afternoon sitting in suffocating silence. As soon as the minute hand ticked its way to four-twenty p.m., Lia rose from the chair, grabbed her backpack, and left the room without another word. It had taken weeks and weeks for the doctor to coax anything out of Lia but silence and disdain, but eventually Lowenstein had succeeded where no one else had. He'd waited Lia out, patient as a rabbit in a burrow. He'd let her spend entire half hours pretend-crying into her hands, then lifting her head to reveal it had all been an act and that she wasn't, in fact, actually sobbing over her terrible fear of clowns, or giant pencils, or anything else she'd come up with that day. Finally, there came a day when Lia had entered the room in a genuine rage. She'd paced like a caged animal, muttering under her breath, and watching the clock desperately. She was hoping it would run out before she cracked and started yelling about what was on her mind. Lowenstein waited her out, calm and silent, and finally Lia had exploded.

"I hate her."

Dr. Lowenstein had looked up at her, blinking, his hands folded in his lap.

"Whom do you hate?"

"My mother. My slimy, insane, manipulative snake of a mother."

"Tell me about her."

So Lia talked. She told the doctor about the call that she'd had with her mother that day—the way she was always trying to convince Ophelia to ask her grandmother for money on her behalf, calling her ungrateful and spoiled.

"She's crazy," said Ophelia. "And I hate the fact that when she's nice to me, I believe her. She's tricked me so many times, and yet . . . when she calls me, and she's being nice, I always want to believe her, even though I know better."

"Parents can be difficult for us to understand sometimes," said Dr. Lowenstein. "You aren't alone in that regard, at least."

That had been the day that changed everything. It hadn't happened in leaps and bounds, even after that breakthrough, but little-by-little, Lia had relaxed around Dr. Lowenstein. She would've thought that having a male psychologist would make things more difficult, but it didn't—he had none of the ego of any of the others, and he didn't treat her like a conquest. Some of the other psychologists had acted like they cared about Lia's well-being, but she could smell the desire on them to add her to their list of accomplishments. Lia was from a wealthy, prominent family, a known problem child—the doctor who could turn her into a well-adjusted and amenable teenager would have a real feather in their cap. Dr. Lowenstein didn't want to make her one of his feathers, and Lia appreciated that about him. It sounded cliché, but he treated her like any other girl, and not like a piece of fragile china, or like a rich girl from a rich family, even though she felt like both of those things at times.

Chapter Six

Dr. Lowenstein handed Lia her ice water with lemon and settled into the high-backed leather chair that he preferred. Lia had taken the smaller one, crossing her legs under her as she sipped the water.

"So," said Dr. Lowenstein, "how was your weekend?"

"It sucked."

"Why's that?"

"I finally moved out of the room I shared with Margot."

"Really?"

Lowenstein glanced up at her over his glasses.

"Yeah, really."

"I thought you liked Margot."

"I do like Margot."

"Then why the move?"

"I can't say exactly. It just wasn't working. She has issues that I can't . . . be around."

Lia didn't feel comfortable telling Lowenstein the details of the reasoning behind her move. It had taken her days and subtle bribing of several prefects to even get the room transfer approved, and the fact that Darlene's roommate had unexpectedly left around the same time was pure happy coincidence. Not for the poor girl herself, maybe, but certainly for Lia. Lowenstein might be a medical professional, so these conversations were private, but he was still a mandated reporter. Lia wasn't going to take any chances by admitting that her ex-roommate was involved in a very illegal sales operation. No—it was better to keep quiet. She didn't want to get Margot into any trouble, either. The girl had enough of her own stuff to figure out.

"Well, I applaud you prioritizing your mental health, then," said the doctor. "That's very responsible of you."

"Hey, I try."

"What else is going on in your life? How are your grades?"

"They're where they need to be," said Lia, running a hand through her hair. "I'll never be a mathematician, but my GPA should be in the right range for me not to get kicked out of school or anything."

"That's good to hear. Have you decided on a piece for the Arts & Design showcase?"

Lia scowled. Dr. Lowenstein raised his hands apologetically, a genial smile spreading across his face.

"Alright, alright, I get it. We don't have to discuss that one."

"I just haven't found anything perfect yet," said Lia. "And none of my ideas are coming out the way I want them to."

"What do you mean?"

"I'm having the artist's version of writer's block,

I guess. I keep trying out new styles, new painting inspirations, but nothing is right. I made that enormous painting, you know, the one I told you about with all the colors? And I tore it in half the next day. I'm at a loss here."

"Sounds like you need some new inspiration."

"I'm plenty inspired. I'm just having trouble translating that to canvas." Lia leaned back, crossing her arms. "Maybe it's all this self-control, Zen stuff you've been teaching me. I bottled up all my real emotions and now I can't create my art anymore."

"I don't think that allowing your natural tendency to let rage reign supreme over your emotions is wise, even for the potential sake of art," said Dr. Lowenstein wryly. "And I also like to think we've made progress toward doing more than just bottling up your emotions. I've seen you come quite a long way since the beginning of the year."

"Thanks, Lowenstein," said Lia, raising her eyebrows. "I'm touched."

"I just don't want you thinking that you need to

be self-destructive to be creative. I don't think that's true at all. I think you're enormously talented in any frame of mind."

"I guess we'll see at the showcase, anyway."

"That we will. You'll come up with something great, Lia."

"I hope so. I'd work on it more this weekend, but its Parents' Weekend."

"I thought your grandmother couldn't attend?"

"She can't."

Lia still felt the cold stab of disappointment. Her grandmother was traveling abroad and had let Lia know she wouldn't be able to make it, but the knowledge still stung. Lia missed her. She hadn't seen her grandmother in months, since she'd come to the school earlier in the year to check on Lia's progress. She called Lia regularly, but it wasn't the same as seeing her in person. Lia had been lucky enough to spend Christmas break with her, avoiding her parents entirely, but her grandmother had left soon after the break ended. Her mom had a fit about Lia missing the holiday at home, as though she wanted to hang out and get pedicures with Lia or something. *Hypocrite.*

"I'm sorry to hear that, Lia," said Dr. Lowenstein. "Isn't there anyone else in your family who could come instead? It's not required, of course, but someone in your situation is encouraged to have their family members be as involved as possible in events like this one. It shows familial support, which is crucial to success at institutes like Beverly Hills Prep."

"Institute? If you mean mental, you've got that absolutely right. Half the girls in this place are totally wacko."

The doctor sighed. His patience for Lia's sense of humor appeared to be low today.

"I just want to make sure that you have family coming if you want to have them here," he said. "What about your parents?"

Lia stiffened, her back arching away from her chair.

"Don't go there," said Lia.

"Why not?"

"Don't give me that. You know why not. Because I hate them both."

The doctor sighed again.

"I understand your feelings, Lia, but I think it might be a good idea. It would be an extension of an olive branch, if you will. You've made great progress this year but one area in which you haven't budged is in regards to your feelings about your parents. Until you let go of this resentment and hatred that you feel toward them, you'll never really be free and clear of their influence on you, and I know how much you want to be independent of them."

Lia shifted uncomfortably in her seat. Inside, she was waging an old war against her head and her heart. Her head urged her to be reasonable. What the doctor was saying seemed practical, and Lia knew that, rationally. It had made sense all year, since the first time she'd heard his advice, but just because something was logical didn't mean it was easy to accept. She understood that it would be much easier to at least attempt to get along with her parents. Lia was still a minor, and young for her year—she wouldn't turn eighteen until a few weeks after she graduated high school, and that was more than a year away. Playing nice with her mother would allow her to ride out the next year or so in relative peace, but Lia's heart wouldn't allow it. Every time someone brought up her mother's name, Lia flinched. The doctor's words were wise ones, she knew that on some level, but a deeper level of her being still wouldn't accept their truth. *Our past goes too deep*, thought Lia. *I'll never be able to let that go.*

"I'll think about it," Lia said. It was the best she could do right now.

Chapter Seven

After her counseling session, Lia went into the nurse's office briefly to participate in the delightful bi-monthly tradition of peeing in a cup for the school's drug-testing requirement.

When she was done, she washed her hands and handed the sample to the nurse with a large, fake smile plastered across her face, as though there was nothing that gave her more joy than this ritual. Nurse Lori just sighed. Lia tended to have that effect on adults.

"When will you guys learn that I don't do drugs?" asked Lia as the nurse labeled her sample and placed it in the storing area to prepare for testing. "I mean, I'll keep doing this for as long as you want—I enjoy it, really, but I can't imagine that testing my pee month after month is any fun for you."

"It's the headmistress's orders, Lia," sighed Nurse Lori. "You know that. Don't take it personally."

"It's difficult not to take it personally when someone is treating you like a criminal," said Lia, "but I'll give it my best shot."

"See you in two weeks, honey."

Lia left the room, grabbing her shoulder bag as she went. They were serving artichoke and shrimp linguine at dinner with roasted asparagus and corn, and chocolate eclairs for dessert.

As Lia trekked across campus all the way back to the dining hall in her dormitory building, she considered Dr. Lowenstein's words. The guy seemed entirely too well-balanced to be a real person, in her opinion, but he always made convincing points. Almost against her will, Lia always found herself considering his advice after their sessions. She didn't want to mess up the progress she'd made this year. She definitely didn't want to go back to being kicked out of schools left and right. Look at how well that had worked out for her in her life so far. But still . . . the thought of trying to reconcile the relationship she had with her parents left a bad taste in her mouth. Even with how far she'd come, Lia wasn't sure she was ready to take that step yet. Shivering now as the outside temperature continued to drop, Lia let herself into her dorm building. It felt like rain. She could almost smell it on the wind. Rain was fine with her—she wasn't really a lounge-in-the-sun type of girl, anyway.

Darlene wasn't in the common room when Lia let herself in. Her bedroom door was open, but she was nowhere in sight. Lia was starting to think that the girl actually lived in the library. She tossed her book bag onto her own bed, ignoring the piles of boxes still waiting to be unpacked. As long as she could clear paths to her desk and to the bathroom, she could avoid unpacking forever. When you wore a uniform every single day of your life, it made it easy to get dressed in the morning with minimal effort. Lia changed from her vest to the soft, long-sleeved shirt that was part of the uniform permitted to be worn by resident students at dinnertime and during Study Hall. It was emblazoned with the Beverly Hills Prep crest, but Lia had added a few flourishes of her own.

As she tugged the shirt over her head, the drawing came into focus—Lia had managed to outline the crest with fabric paint, so that it looked as though the crest were transformed into a lewdly grinning face, complete with horns and a tongue stuck out to the side. It was subtle and artistically done, but Lia had gotten some very prolonged scrutiny whenever she'd worn it, and a few girls had even pointed at her, although they'd all stopped pretty quickly when faced with Lia's glare. Girls might point and whisper, and they might speculate on whether or not she was actually psycho, but none were brave enough to actually confront her—except Grace, of course. Just thinking of her made Lia scowl. She pulled her hair into a high ponytail and headed to dinner. Maybe four helpings of pasta would help improve her mood.

Two hours later, stuffed to the brim with pasta, shrimp, and what must have been at least a pound of eclairs, Lia was slow to open the door to the prefect who was checking her into Study Hall. The prefect was a frazzled-looking brunette with the ubiquitous clipboard. She avoided Lia's gaze, staring at the tops of her shoes the entire time she talked to her. *She's terrified of me,* thought Lia, with a touch of irritation. *What, does she think I'm going to turn her into a frog or something?*

"Do you have a laptop permission slip?" the girl asked.

"Sure do."

Lia produced the crumpled note from her literature teacher, which basically just said that Lia had homework to do that would require laptop usage, and that Lia wasn't going to use her computer to do something stupid, like watch YouTube videos during Study Hall. The rules here about computer usage were strict, but Lia had seen girls work their way around the firewalls and spend the entire Study Hall period on Instagram anyway. Then, the school had started disabling the Wi-Fi entirely during Study Hall, which definitely put a wrench in things considering they also required some resident students to turn over their phones during that time, but it was a temporary lull. It seemed to Lia that it would be a lot easier to just accept the fact that the girls were going to be on the internet on their tablets or laptops, but whatever. It wasn't her issue to worry about.

The prefect squinted at her slip and nodded, checking Lia's name off on the list on her clipboard. Lia handed her cell phone to the prefect, who would return it after the Study Hall period. It was part of her agreement with the school, one of the only parts that Lia didn't mind. There was no one that she really wanted to talk to besides her grandmother, anyway, and Lenore had only recently started to grasp the concept of email.

"Are we done?" said Lia.

"Oh, yeah. You're all set."

"Peachy," said Lia, and she shut the door again.

Since Darlene was still AWOL and would probably be holed up in one of the libraries studying, Lia grabbed a blanket and prepared to curl up on the couch and work on her homework. She'd saved a bunch of images onto her computer earlier in the day to flip through, too, for inspiration for some new drawings she was trying to create—winter landscapes, some of her favorite portrait photographers' work. Something had to be the inspiration for a new piece. She just had to find her muse. It was starting to irritate her that nothing she was making seemed right. Her teachers seemed to like her pieces just fine; she got perfect grades on the ones that she submitted, and the ones she had listed as possibilities for her AP portfolio for this year were deemed excellent in terms of technical detail. But they were just okay, to Lia, not great, and she needed something great to display in spring.

Her best work, or at least her own favorite pieces, were the ones that were inspired by her own dreams. Sometimes she'd wake in the middle of the night, grab a pencil and wildly sketch an abstract vision that the next morning would look insane, but in a super cool way. Once, she'd woken up and immediately sketched a woman holding a baby girl and smiling, another time it was a meadow of wildflowers and a stream, and another time it had been a vast ocean filled with fantastical mermaids. That particular sketch had gotten more than a few second glances when she'd hung it up in class. But, it had been a while since she'd had a dream she remembered, for whatever reason. Maybe it was stress or something. Sighing, Lia propped her feet on the George VII coffee table and tried to get her mind to focus on Shakespeare for the time being.

Chapter Eight

The next two hours passed quickly enough. With the help of Motörhead blasting from her headphones, Lia had made some progress on her *Romeo and Juliet* essay, even though she hated the play. *Hamlet* was her top choice—who didn't love a story about family members killing each other? Darlene barged in right as the Study Hall period ended. She barely glanced at Lia, marching straight to her room, an open book under her nose that she flipped through furiously as she walked.

Freak, thought Lia, rolling her eyes.

There was another knock on the door. Lia got

up and went to retrieve her phone from the prefect, powering it on again to see if she'd missed any messages from her grandmother. Instead, two missed calls popped up. Lia sat back down on the couch as she clicked on the icon, expecting Grandmamma's number to show up. Instead, Lia frowned as her mother's number showed on her missed call list.

Why is Sonia calling me?

Lia shrugged to herself and tossed her phone across the couch, plugging her headphones back into her ears. She hadn't talked to her mother on the phone for months. Sonia had tried a few times after Lia was enrolled at Beverly Hills Prep, but every call had ended up being a screaming match, with Sonia crying on one end of the line and Lia throwing things across the room on the other. Eventually, the calls had stopped, or were at least on hiatus, and Lia had been absolutely fine with that. Casual chats with her mother would never be a frequent cornerstone of her life; the two of them were just too different.

Since she was little, Lia had been aware that her

mother didn't act like other moms did. Rarely did she hug Lia or play with her—for the most part she left her with nannies and maids while she spent hours away from the house, returning with bags and bags of designer clothes—and bags of prescription bottles freshly filled from the pharmacy. When she was home, she was fighting with Lia's father or curled up in her enormous four-poster bed, sleeping for what seemed like days at a time. Lia couldn't count the number of nights she'd crept from her bedroom as a child, gray eyes enormous in her pale face, and hidden behind the staircase railing on the second floor to listen to her parents fighting in the library.

The old house—where Lia had been born in the third-floor bedroom in the family tradition that she found revolting—was so big that sometimes it took Lia ten minutes to follow her parents' voices to whatever wing they were fighting in. Lia knew every inch of the enormous estate on the edge of the ocean, far away on the East Coast. Her earliest memory was of a sunbeam shining through the floor-to-ceiling window in the east wing office; her second earliest was of the main library, the rows and rows of books and the paintings on the walls that she would sit and stare at for hours when she'd run from her nanny to hide. Lia's earliest memories of her mother were of a woman with angry eyes and hands that had a tendency to slap and pinch or wrestle Lia back into a dress that she hated.

"You want to be mommy's pretty princess, don't you?" she'd croon to her, shoving Lia's arms into navy satin sleeves on the rare occasion that she'd dressed Lia herself. That mostly happened when there was an event of some kind that Sonia wanted to attend and show Lia off. Lia had gone sullenly to Daughters of the American Revolution meetings, cotillions, parties, and whatever else her mother had dragged her to, hating every second of it. She hated the fake smiles and the way the adults all pretended to be polite to one another, and the way she and the rest of the progeny were paraded around like little porcelain dolls, expected to act like perfect miniatures of their parents. Sonia and Lia had begun to fight, too, very early on.

Lia's only solace had been in her grandmother. She was the only person who Sonia seemed to listen to, more out of fear than anything else. There was a time that Lia remembered, in which she couldn't have been more than four or five, that Lia had one of her first memories of her grandmother. Her mother was out of bed and for some reason she had woken up angry and called for Lia, who was hiding from one of her nannies. Lia had huddled into the tiniest ball she could manage behind an enormous armchair in the library, trying not to breathe, but her mother had found her and grabbed one of her ankles, and Lia had started to scream. Her mother was thin as a rail, her mouth a twisted line of anger, dark hair flying wildly like a tornado. Without her makeup on and her hair done, she looked tired and frantic. Then her grandmother had walked in the door, and everything went quiet. Lia had lain on the floor, sobbing, and her grandmother had crossed to her and picked her up, calming her with a gentle touch of her hand. To her daughter, she directed a withering stare. From then on, they'd been each other's favorites.

Lia's grandmother, Lenore Sonia Koroleva, was directly descended from an ancient line of Romanov royalty. She was the only child of Lia's great-grandfather, who had left her an enormous fortune when he died when Sonia was a teenager. Lia understood that Sonia had been raised in the same world in which she raised Lia; they'd had the same opportunities, the same time in the same social circles. But, somehow, they'd turned out as differently from each other as two people could possibly be. Lia had eschewed almost every aspect of that socialite world since she was old enough to say the word "no." She wasn't stupid—she enjoyed the privileges that came with being born into her family, to a certain extent. She'd never protested against being taken on trips with her grandmother to Italy, the Caribbean, and France. Having come from money, she was used to a certain standard of life, and she knew not everyone in the world had the opportunities she did. But she shunned any part of that world that didn't seem genuine to her.

Avoiding the social spotlight had made Lia a sort of pariah in that world, completely unlike the other daughters and sons born into opportunity, who did things like steal yachts and blow through hundreds of thousands of dollars on anything at all. While her grandmother was content to let Lia live as she pleased, it made her mother irate. Sonia relied on Lia in regards to their social status. In a family like theirs, daughters were a direct reflection of their mothers. If Lia couldn't even be bothered to do the most basic social requirements, like attending a coming out cotillion to be presented to society, or being sworn in as a Daughter of the American Revolution, then Sonia would be looked upon as a bad mother. And that was a slight that Sonia couldn't bear. At least, that's how she phrased it to Lia, and Lia reacted with a temper of her own. Over the years, the feud had grown deeper as Lia had moved from school to school, constantly in trouble. She wasn't sure there could ever be peace.

Lia looked back down at her phone, flipping it over in her hands. It would be safer, undoubtedly, to ignore this. There was no compelling reason she should call her mother back, although she wished that Sonia had left a voicemail so Lia would know if anything was seriously wrong. She'd probably avoided leaving one on purpose. Lia set her phone down on the coffee table, sliding it away from her, and leaned forward so her chin rested in her hands. As her phone laid there, Lia tried to think of something besides what her mother could have been calling about. Could it have been her dad calling from her mom's phone? He was never with her; he preferred to work long hours at the insurance firm where he practically lived. Lia would never understand how he'd wound up marrying her mother, someone so completely different than him.

Lia eyed her phone, picked it up, and set it down again. Darlene was going over flashcards in her bedroom; the sound of her voice repeating phrases over and over was grating on Lia's nerves. Lia picked up her phone and pressed the last number on her Missed Calls list. Her heart immediately leapt into her throat, but she bit her lip and listened to her mother's phone ring. Maybe it would go straight to voicemail, and she could leave a message, and then when her mother called back she could let it go to voicemail too and they could communicate that way. Just as the last ring buzzed in her ear and the pressure on her chest started to ease, Lia heard a click.

"Ophelia, darling?"

Her mother's voice.

Chapter Nine

"Um, hi. Hi Mom."

"Hello, Ophelia, dear."

Lia winced. This was a very, very weird mood. "Dear" was not a word often used by her mother in reference to her only child.

"You called me," said Lia lamely. "I was just returning your call."

"Right. Well, I wanted to see if you were aware that this coming weekend is Parents' Weekend at your school."

What in the world?

"Yeah Mom, it's Parents' Weekend this weekend. So what?"

"Well, were you planning on letting me know?"

"I didn't think you'd want to come, Mom."

"Why would you think that?" Her tone was light and airy, like she was speaking to a beloved child with whom she'd never even consider raising her voice to. It made Lia suspicious.

"Well, I don't know—maybe because you haven't been here since I moved in last fall? Because the last time I really talked to you was when I was telling you that I wasn't coming home for Christmas Break. When I said I was going to stay with Grandmamma instead, you freaked out."

"I don't recall that at all," said Sonia breezily, dismissing Lia's words as casually as if she were shooing away a mosquito. "I know how much you like to be dramatic."

"Right," said Lia. "So when you screamed at me that I was an ungrateful child with no respect for my family and that I was purposefully doing this to hurt you—that wasn't you?"

"I just think you're remembering it wrong. It was just a little disagreement, Ophelia, that's it."

"Mom, let's just move on." Lia rubbed a hand across her forehead; her mother was in fine form tonight.

"As you wish," said Sonia, apparently happy to oblige for once. "As I was saying, this coming weekend is Parents' Weekend and I think it's only right that you have a parent attending."

"Just you? No Dad?"

It was a rhetorical question. Lia hadn't seen her parents in the same room together without someone screaming in about a decade.

"I think he's busy at work," said her mother with just a touch of frost.

"I figured as much."

"So, can you spare a day for your mother? I can stay at the beach house in Newport. It shouldn't take too long to call the maid service in Beverly Hills and have them send a team to spruce it up."

Lia didn't know what to say. "No" would be her safest answer, and would save her from whatever insanity her mom was planning. But, knowing her mother, she'd show up anyway and the last thing Lia wanted was some sort of scene. There was an angle here that she was missing, but for the life of her she couldn't see what it was. What could her mother possibly get out of coming to Parents' Weekend? It was just a dumb event with a few activities so that parents could come and gloat over how great their mediocre kids were. It didn't seem like Sonia's sort of gig.

"Sure," was what Lia ended up saying, and as soon as she said it, she had the terrible feeling that she'd live to regret it.

Oh, stop it, Lia told herself as her mom babbled on about what they'd do while she was visiting. *Dr. Lowenstein thinks this sort of reconciliation would be a good idea. This is a good idea.*

So why couldn't she shake the feeling that she'd just been tricked?

Lia hung up about fifteen minutes later feeling no closer to the truth. Rarely had phone conversations with her mother gone as smoothly as that one had. It was like Sonia had thirteen different personalities just waiting to pop out at any given time. Even after sixteen years, Lia couldn't pin her down.

She gave up trying to keep studying. During Study Hall she'd gotten a good amount done on her essay, even though she was nowhere close to finding a new inspiration for her Art & Design showcase piece. That one was still eluding her. It was getting late; going to bed and sleeping off the weirdness of the night seemed like her best option at this point. Leaving the blanket in a pile on the couch, Lia opened her bedroom door and flipped the lights on so she could dig out her favorite oversized *Game of Thrones* T-shirt with Daenerys Targaryen's face on it to sleep in. She washed her face and let her hair down from her ponytail and then crawled right into her sheets and tugged the comforter to her chin. The room was dark, and quiet, and Lia felt her body relaxing, but her mind was whirring at warp speed. Closing her eyes, she tried to take slow deep breaths to calm her thoughts down, but it was a long time of tossing and turning before she got to sleep.

For the rest of the week, Lia tried to forget about the looming weekend ahead of her. She dutifully worked on her essay and other schoolwork, she got a solid C on an Algebra II exam, and she avoided Grace everywhere she went. A few times, she passed Margot in the hallway or glimpsed her in the dining hall, and she didn't like what she saw. Margot, already slender, was looking thin and there was something about her eyes that Lia didn't like. It was familiar, somehow. She looked jumpy and preoccupied. Lia wished that she could help, but every time she even started in Margot's direction, she could feel Grace's stare practically penetrating her spine. Grace definitely didn't want the two of them together, and Lia didn't want Grace harassing her or Margot anymore. Maybe if she let Margot be, Grace would leave both of them alone. So, Lia stayed away, and hoped that would help.

She had another counseling appointment Thursday afternoon, and Dr. Lowenstein commented on her distractedness.

"I'm just nervous about this weekend," Lia admitted. "I haven't seen my mother in months, and then this phone call out of the blue? It's just not like her. Usually she'd come up with some sort of devious plan to get me to call her first, and then she would apply a guilt trip so that I felt obligated to invite her. This was too straightforward. It was weird."

"The lines of communication between the two of you are certainly convoluted," said Dr. Lowenstein. "But I think you should be considering giving your mother the benefit of the doubt here."

"What? You traitor."

"Isn't it possible that your mother just wanted to come and visit you? You've been doing incredibly well here, and making wonderful progress. Maybe she wants to see it for herself, and enjoy it."

"Oh, she wants to enjoy something alright," said Lia darkly. "But I don't think she's coming to congratulate me on my GPA."

The doctor sighed, sitting back in his chair.

"Your skepticism toward your mother's intentions hurts you more than it hurts her, Lia. Unless you give her the chance to be there for you, to come see you for no other reason than to have a nice weekend, the door will never open up between you two. Your mother has extended an olive branch of her own. She sounds like she wants to visit, and she wants to see you. I think that's a very promising start toward repairing the holes in that relationship."

"I don't want to repair any holes," muttered Lia. "I like it just fine when I stay on my side, and she stays on hers, and no one comes to the middle. These past few months without talking to her have been so calm."

"Do you really think it would be so bad to have her come? I appreciate the way she was straightforward in her call to you. There was none of that passive aggression you talk so much about."

"Not this time, at least."

"I don't want you to rush into anything that you're not ready for," said Dr. Lowenstein. "If you feel as though you need more time to adjust, or that you truly don't want her to come, then maybe you should tell her to stay home. I will say that telling her not to come might make you feel more comfortable, but if you go that route, you'll be in the same place you are now. Your relationship won't move forward at all; it will stay just the way it is currently, or perhaps get worse."

"Look, you don't know my mother," said Lia. "You don't know which way she'll turn at any given minute. I could wind up taking our relationship backward three big, giant steps over the course of this weekend. You can't predict what will happen."

"You're right, Lia, of course. But neither can you. You have to allow yourself to take a chance, to see what happens. Or don't—as I said, I truly think it's your choice. But I would be glad to see you taking steps toward improving the relationship between your mother and yourself. I think it would help your personal well-being enormously to resolve some of the conflicts lingering between you two."

Lia just shook her head. Yeah, resolving conflicts was great, but in her entire lifetime there had been no resolving of anything when it came to her mother. There was fighting, and plenty of passive aggression, and occasionally a frigid silence or two, but not much issue resolution. But maybe the doctor was right— maybe she had to give her mother a chance to see if her intentions were good. Lia crossed her legs, considering the situation. She really had come a long way since she'd been at this school. Maybe now she could handle herself more like an adult, and communicate with her mom like the other girls managed to with their own mothers.

"I'll try," muttered Lia reluctantly, after a few minutes of silence. "I don't know what will happen, or if it will work, but I'll try."

"I'm very glad to hear that, Lia. I think this is a step in a very positive direction."

"Yeah, yeah."

"What time does your mother arrive?"

"She's supposed to get to our house in Newport Beach around eleven tomorrow morning, and then come here for the brunch and the tour of the grounds."

"Splendid."

"I guess so."

"Well, that's our time," said Dr. Lowenstein, rising from his chair. "We'll check in Monday afternoon and see how the weekend went."

"I'm already looking forward to it," sighed Lia, giving him a reluctant, but hopeful, smile.

Chapter Ten

Lia could have very well been expelled based solely on the amount of demerits she'd receive at Saturday morning inspection, if she didn't have an exemption because of her recent move. The dorm head actually gasped when she saw the mounds of boxes and clothes still strewn about Lia's room. She'd tried to clean a little, considering her mom was here and might actually see her room for the first time, but the floor was still cluttered with boxes. There were piles of paintbrushes and crumpled uniform skirts and about a thousand pairs of shoes that Lia hadn't managed to shove into a closet yet, but overall she thought it was a big improvement.

"I understand your exemption this time," said the flustered dorm head, "but next week this all needs to be cleaned up, or I'm going to have to give you demerits."

"Next week, all of this will be gone," said Lia, nudging a box of her painting clothes out of the way with her toe. "I swear. Anyway, it still looks way better than it did when I first got all my stuff in here. I unpacked like half of my boxes last night."

"There's still a lot of progress to be made," said the dorm head, shaking her head. She left the room to complete the inspection of the other half of the suite, and Lia shrugged. It didn't look that bad to her. Opening her closet doors, Lia took out the navy dress that she'd chosen for today. The uniform wasn't required at weekend events, thank goodness, but there was still a business-casual dress code that would be enforced. The dress was Valentino, a dark blue with long sleeves and a high neck, an empire waist—and all covered in delicate lace. Lia thought it brought out the blue in her gray eyes. Choosing tights and a pair of low-heeled leather booties made from buttery Italian leather, Lia moved to the bathroom to do her hair and makeup. She wore thrift store finds as often as she wore designers, but today she wanted to look nice.

It felt sort of silly to get this dressed up just to see her mom, but Lia hadn't seen her in months. The occasion seemed to warrant a little extra effort, so Lia curled her dark hair until it hung in soft waves halfway down her back, and she smudged on just a hint of liner and shadow. Light makeup was allowed, or more like tolerated, on weekends for resident students. Lia chose a diamond solitaire necklace that had been a gift from her grandmother, and put on earrings to match. She'd finally gotten an email from her grandmother the night before. It had taken a solid hour to read through the entire thing on her laptop and respond. After her grandmother apologized for not being in better contact with Lia, Lenore had then gone on for almost two pages about the renovations she was overseeing at the family estate somewhere in the English countryside. Lia had smiled as she read along:

I wish you could see the sort of situation I'm dealing with here, darling. The entire west wing of this place has been allowed to fall into total disrepair and it seems as though I'm the only one who has an idea of what needs to be done. When this project is finished we'll take a trip here and visit some of the museums, and I'll see if I can make an English horsewoman of you yet.

The headmistress sent me another update on your progress. It sounds like you're doing wonderfully, Lia . . .

While Lia seriously doubted that the renovation team was incompetent, she did know that no one had standards as high as her grandmother's. Lia had tried telling her that any of her assistants could've gone abroad to oversee the project, but no one could do anything perfectly for Lenore. Lia had caught her going to each bedroom in her Connecticut estate and re-making the beds after the maids. The woman was tireless, and intimidating—Lia was the only person who was almost never on the receiving end of Lenore Koroleva's temper. How in the world had she convinced Headmistress Chambers to send her updates on Lia? She wasn't even Lia's legal guardian, but somehow, Lia wasn't surprised. Tracing the diamond on her necklace, Lia sighed. She missed her grandmother. She could've used her support today.

Checking her watch, Lia realized it was already ten to eleven; she needed to get to the Great Hall to meet her mother for Parents' Weekend brunch. Lia blew out a nervous breath and chose a soft cashmere sweater to wear over her dress before leaving her room. Darlene had left early this morning. Lia had no idea if she was studying all day or if her parents were here, too. Maybe she had a normal family and her mother and father would both show up together. *A normal family,* thought Lia wryly. *What a concept.*

By the time Lia made it to the Great Hall, the foyer was already starting to fill up with girls and their families. Lia made her way awkwardly through the crowd, excusing herself as she went, so that she could get a spot near to the door. She checked her phone but there had been no texts from her mother. Knowing her, she'd changed her mind and decided not to come and just didn't let Lia know. Biting her lip, Lia eyed the entrance to Beverly Hills Prep nervously. More families congregated, parents and grandparents coming through the doorway to be greeted by daughters and granddaughters eagerly leading them inside. Lia sighed and rolled her eyes, tapping her foot impatiently on the marble floor. *Where in the world is Sonia?*

Then, as though she'd conjured her up with that very thought, there she was.

Sonia walked through the door and it was like the atmosphere immediately changed. Lia would have sworn that every person in that room turned to look, as though she were exuding some kind of electromagnetic field. Wives looked her over with jealousy. Girls eyed her clothing, which was impeccable, from the YSL boots to the Birkin bag on her slender arm.

Sonia smiled, enjoying the attention that Lia had seen her receive since Lia was a child, and then her eyes lit on Lia's. Where Lia had worked her way through the crowd like a salmon swimming upstream, people seemed to just part for Sonia, so that she reached Lia with minimal effort, taking her hands in her own slim ones. Her wedding ring sat on her left hand, glittering with a solitaire as big as a nickel. Sonia's hands were soft and smooth, her nails perfectly manicured, painted a flawless nude. Lia's were bitten and one nail was still painted hot pink. But from her long, dark hair to the gray eyes, Lia knew they could pass for sisters. It had happened before, to Sonia's obvious delight.

"Ophelia, honey," murmured Sonia, leaning closer to kiss Lia's cheek, "how are you? You look thin." She stepped back a little to appraise Lia critically, and Lia knew the last sentence had been meant as a compliment. Lia looked her mother over, too. She looked the same as she always did, dressed to the nines, like she was straight out of a catalog—but Lia didn't like the restless look in her expression. Her hands shook as they released Lia's, another warning sign.

"I eat just as much as ever, Mom. And I'm fine. How are you?"

"Well, I'm doing alright," said Sonia. "Traveling here was quite the pain, I can attest to that."

"You flew?"

"Of course. I took the jet. I mean, the traffic from the Newport Beach house to here—I thought I'd be stuck between two minivans for the rest of my life."

"Sorry you hit traffic, Mom."

"Oh, it's not a problem, dear."

Sonia linked her arm through Lia's and guided her past the other girls and their families into the foyer of the Great Hall.

"So, this is the school that your grandmother insisted you attend."

"She just wanted me to go somewhere good, Mom. There weren't a ton of other options."

Sonia shrugged elegantly, her silky hair sliding over her shoulder. "It'll do, I guess."

Sonia kept up a steady flow of small talk as Lia walked her through the Great Hall and down the corridor toward the banquet room where brunch was being held. The banquet room was enormous, with vaulted ceilings and gold edgings on the doorways and the windowsills. Brunch was buffet-style, and there were two long tables covered in trays of muffins, croissants, toast, fruit, coffee, and tea. There was enough food to feed a small army for a year, but Sonia ate lightly as always, filling a china plate with strawberries and half an English muffin and not much else. Lia grabbed as much as she could fit on her plate, adding a giant cup of coffee to the mix while she was at it. She hadn't had breakfast yet, and she was hungry.

Sonia led them to an empty table for two underneath the crystal chandelier. There was a makeshift stage set up near the front of the room where Lia assumed the headmistress or someone else was planning on speaking. The room was filling up rapidly with other girls and their parents; a lot of them glanced at Sonia, and Lia found herself torn between reluctant admiration for her mother's beauty and irritation generated by the attention Sonia always seemed to garner whenever they were in public. It was a familiar set of emotions for her.

"Is that your headmistress?" Sonia asked, nodding toward Headmistress Chambers, who had entered the room and was in conversation with a set of parents.

"Yeah, that's her."

Sonia eyed her like a hawk eyeing a mouse, and Lia frowned slightly.

"She looks strict. That's good for you."

Now Lia rolled her eyes. But she bit her tongue, and did what Dr. Lowenstein would have recommended: she pictured a calm sea. Getting mad at her mom had historically terrible consequences. The woman had a temper worse than Lia's, and that was saying something.

"I can see why you like this place so much," said Sonia, sipping her black tea. "It's certainly lavish. The cost of your tuition alone—"

"You're not even paying for my tuition, Mom," snapped Lia. "What do you care what it costs?"

Sonia's eyes flashed for a moment, and then a cold smile tilted her lips at the corners, but she didn't say anything. The headmistress stepped up on the podium, and the room went quiet. Headmistress Chambers could quiet a room full of adults just as quickly as a room full of teenagers, evidently.

"Welcome, parents, friends, and family," the headmistress began, "to Beverly Hills Preparatory Academy. We're thrilled that you could join us for the 92nd annual Parents' Weekend. We're tremendously proud of all these young ladies and the accomplishments they attain within these halls. For many years, this school has been a beacon as a destination of choice for exemplary young women looking for the best opportunities that a school can provide. We like to think that, with your generous assistance of course, we prove the reputation that has been built through the years."

Polite applause filled the banquet room, and the

headmistress continued into her welcome speech. As Lia settled into her chair with a mouthful of cherry Danish, her mother reached casually into her Birkin bag, and pulled out her phone.

"I'll be right back," her mother said, and she swept out of the room, leaving her purse half-open on the chair next to Lia. As the doors to the banquet room clicked shut again, Lia realized her mother hadn't said where she was going. Lia frowned, then leaned forward, eyeing her mother's purse. She shouldn't look inside. It was a violation of privacy. Sonia would hate it, she always hated it when Lia used to go into her bedroom or look through her closet, playing spy as a child. Years of ingrained manners kept Lia still for another thirty seconds, and then she couldn't take it anymore. Glancing back at the door, Lia tugged the purse toward her so she could see inside, and then breathed a sigh of relief. There was nothing in the purse but her mother's wallet, a phone charger, and about a thousand of the tea packets she drank constantly. *Is this how paranoid I am?* Lia asked herself. *I'm searching through her stuff now?* Lia wasn't sure why she felt as though her mother would have a loaded gun or something in there, but she was relieved to see that she appeared to be prepared to be on her best behavior today. Lia hadn't thought it was possible, but hope bloomed in her chest that this would be a good day.

Chapter Eleven

Lia quickly shoved the purse back into its spot on the chair and continued listening to the headmistress, crossing and uncrossing her legs anxiously. She wanted so badly to believe that everything would go smoothly today, but she was afraid to trust Sonia, despite the fact that she seemed genuinely normal this morning.

Maybe it would be fine. Her mom had been nothing but genial since her arrival, except for that weird comment about the headmistress. Sonia was volatile on her best days, though. Lia could never really pin down what she would do next.

Sonia slid back into her seat and smiled at Lia, who smiled back. Lia continued biting her nails. The headmistress wrapped up the welcome speech and Lia sighed with relief; the room was starting to feel very small.

"Please enjoy a tour of the grounds and school buildings from our team of tour guides. I will also be present to answer any questions anyone might have. Dinner will be served here this evening at five o'clock. Welcome to Beverly Hills Preparatory Academy."

There was more polite applause, and then the groups dispersed as the families sitting at the tables rose and started following the tour guides out of the banquet room.

"Let's go in this group," said Lia to her mother. "She has the least annoying voice."

"Whatever you want, dear."

Lia bit her lip and tried to smile, but her stomach was in knots. She tried to gauge her mom's mood, but Sonia continued to chatter about the pleasant weather and the architecture of the buildings as though she hadn't a care in the world. But a nagging feeling of worry settled over Lia, and she was having trouble dispelling it.

The tour guides took their group over the Beverly Hills Prep grounds. They walked through the arboretum and visited the tennis courts, then took a brief look around the gymnastics and dance annex and the sports teams' state-of-the-art locker rooms. Then they visited the mathematics and science buildings and the brand new auditorium and library. Lia wasn't particularly interested in what wallpaper they'd chosen to decorate the walls with, but her mother seemed riveted. She even asked the tour guide a couple of questions while they were being guided through the Clara Barton Library and again at the plaque with the letter from President John Adams. As the afternoon went on, Lia relaxed. Her mom wasn't being difficult. She was acting as normal as Lia had ever seen her. Maybe everything would end up being okay.

"My goodness, what time is it?" said Sonia as the group finished the tour of the administrative offices.

"This has been so entertaining that I've completely lost track of time."

"It's almost time for dinner," said Lia, checking her watch. "Thank goodness. I'm too hungry to look at any more of the sixteenth century paintings, even if they are exquisite originals."

Sonia laughed lightly, and the two of them walked arm in arm with the rest of the groups back to the Great Hall. The banquet room had been redone completely in the time that the tours were taking place, and long tables had been laid out with deeply cushioned chairs at every place setting.

"You don't have to stay if you're tired, Mom," said Lia. "I mean, if you need to get back to the house, that's fine."

"I'm fine, Ophelia. I'm happy to sit and have dinner with my daughter."

"Well, okay, then," said Lia, smiling. This had gone so unbelievably well.

For dinner they were served a soup and salad course, followed by appetizers, then the entrée, then another salad, and then finally dessert. Lia happily dug into Caesar salad and a rich minestrone, oysters on the half shell as an appetizer, and then filet mignon with scalloped potatoes and a roasted broccolini and coconut salad, topped with turmeric dressing. Waiters served everyone their plates in crisp uniforms, refilling water glasses and bringing dessert after dessert in seemingly endless waves. Lia watched someone's father ask for a third serving of the pudding with a wave of his hand; everyone was becoming more jovial as the meal went on. Sonia sipped delicately on cranberry juice with lime, and seemed calm and even-keeled, chatting pleasantly with Lia as the waiters brought their courses. Lia was in a state of euphoric disbelief at how well the day had gone so far. She'd even enjoyed herself a little, walking around with her mother like every other student there.

The noise in the room grew, and as people finished their desserts, standing groups formed as the adults continued their conversations with glasses in hand. The headmistress and other faculty were making the rounds within the groups. Lia figured this had to be the best time to be chatting with the parents of resident students—they'd been impressed by the tour of the school, and then fed until they were stuffed. There wasn't a better time to be mingling with parents, many of whom were huge donators to the school. More checks would be written tonight, and more money donated to Beverly Hills Prep. Lia was sure that the headmistress was disappointed not to see Lia's grandmother here. She was among the biggest investors, even though it had been necessary for her to make a sizable donation just to get Lia into the school at all. Still, Lia figured it counted.

"I'm going to find the restroom again, Ophelia," said Sonia, and Lia nodded.

"Sure, Mom, I'll be here. I want to see if they can give me another serving of the chocolate pudding."

Sonia nodded and breezed away.

"Excuse me, dear. I love that dress you're wearing," said the middle-aged woman next to Lia. "What a pretty shade of blue."

"Oh, thank you."

As the woman chatted next to her, Lia became aware of a familiar voice in the background of the room. She tried to focus on what the woman seated next to her was chattering about, but it became harder to focus as the familiar voice increased in volume. *Is my mom back from the restroom?*

Lia turned around in her chair, trying to locate the source of the voices. Her mother was standing across the room, in conversation with the headmistress. *What in the world was going on? Did she just feel like having a chat with her?* Her mother was smiling widely, touching the headmistress on the shoulder and tilting her head to the side in the way that always got her what she wanted. The headmistress smiled, nodded, and Lia relaxed—it looked like they were just having a conversation. No big deal. As she watched, the headmistress's polite smile began to fade, and Lia gave up all pretense of listening to whatever the woman next to her was saying. Something was going on. Her mother wasn't smiling anymore, either; her arms were folded and there was a familiar, stubborn set to her chin that chilled Lia's bones.

Lia stood up from the table, grabbed her mom's purse, and made her way through the crowd, intent on separating her mother from the headmistress. Why hadn't she kept better track of what Sonia was doing, and who she was talking to?

Because I shouldn't have to do that, said a nasty little voice in Lia's head. *I shouldn't have to watch her. She's the mother, not me.*

By the time Lia neared her mother, Sonia's voice was beginning to carry throughout the room. People were starting to stare.

"Mom?" said Lia, her hand on her shoulder. "What's going on?"

"Good evening, Lia," said the headmistress, not unkindly, but her eyes, directed on Sonia, were icy.

"Good evening, headmistress."

"We are not through discussing this," said Sonia to the headmistress through clenched teeth, ignoring Lia completely. Her eyes were wild and angry, her hands balled into fists. "That's my family's money that you're stealing and I won't let you get away with it."

"I can assure you, Mrs. Koroleva, that neither I nor this school have stolen anything from you."

"That's a lie. That money came directly from my inheritance, and you took it illegally. You'll be hearing from my lawyer, and we'll have to see if Ophelia will even continue as a student here."

"What?" Panicked, Lia looked from her mother to the headmistress. "Mom, what are you talking about?"

"This entire evening has been disgraceful," said Sonia, and now people were really starting to stare. Lia stayed rooted to the floor, at a total loss. Her mother's worst outbursts generally happened in the privacy of their own home, not at events like this. Not in front of this many people; it just wasn't what the Korolevas did.

"I'm sorry you feel that way," said the headmistress calmly.

"Mom, please, can we just go outside or something?" said Lia in a low voice. "People are staring."

"I don't care if there are people staring or not. This is outrageous, and I won't stand for it."

Lia watched helplessly as her mom continued to throw the equivalent of an adult tantrum over something Lia didn't even understand. She was making grandiose statements veiled thinly by a layer of panic—nothing Lia hadn't seen before, but why here? *Why did it have to be here, and now?*

"Mom, come on," said Lia finally, and she gripped Sonia's wrist and dragged her through the crowd of people, away from the headmistress who had stood calmly with her hands clasped the entire time, and away from the girls who were already starting to whisper about Lia. Lia shoved her mom through the doors and pushed them shut behind her back, her temper flaring.

"Mom, what is going on? Why were you harassing the headmistress? Have you lost your mind?"

"This is your grandmother's fault," seethed Sonia,

who was already pacing on the marble floor of the foyer. Her gaze lit on Lia, as though she were seeing her for the first time.

"Mom, will you please try to calm down?"

"Don't tell me what to do! You're my child, Ophelia."

"Fine!" Lia screamed, the last of her patience fading rapidly. "Fine, Mom, go ahead. I'll just stand here and watch you act like a complete psycho, like always. Is this what you want? To stand here and fight with me in the foyer of my school?"

"Your school?" scoffed Sonia. "Your school? Oh, well, excuse me. I didn't realize you had such deep ties to this place. As I recall it, we practically had to force you to attend."

"You wouldn't know anything about it. Grandmamma was the one who got me in here."

"Don't talk to me about that woman right now," Sonia snarled. "Your grandmother is the reason for all of this." Their voices were practically echoing from the ceilings, and Lia struggled to get her emotions under control.

"Mom, please," said Lia, "don't you want to go somewhere else?"

"No! I pay for you to go here, and I can stand here in the foyer and yell if I like!"

"Fine, you psycho, fine. And Grandmamma paid for this, not you."

"That's what she told you, at least," said Sonia. "But that money should have gone to me."

"Dad has a job, Mom, and you have the trust fund that Grandmamma gave you when you turned twenty-five. There was enough money in that account to give you everything until the day you died, even if Dad never spent another day at that office."

"It's all gone," said Sonia. "All of it. You think your father makes any money? He doesn't even bother to go to the office anymore. He puts on his suit every morning and goes to the club or the casino, like some kind of criminal. It's disgusting."

"You spent your entire trust fund?" For a moment,

Lia was stunned. The information about her father, however, was unsurprising. Lia didn't blame him if what her mother said was true; he'd been worn down by her for so many years. He was such a non-presence in her life anyway that he was as good as a stranger to her. Sonia had never even taken his last name, and hadn't given it to Lia either, when she was born. "Even if you did, I know Grandmamma feeds you and Dad money all the time."

"Is that what she tells you?" Sonia asked.

"It's what I know," said Lia.

"You don't know anything," said Sonia, laughing. "That woman spoils you endlessly, and she leaves me with nothing. Her own daughter."

"Mom, I hardly think you have nothing. You're wearing Fendi, for goodness' sake."

"You always defend her. Even after everything I've done for you," Sonia spat.

"What have you done for me, exactly? Besides mess me up beyond all measure?" Lia accused.

"Oh, don't you dare blame me for your problems.

I didn't get you kicked out of all those schools. You did that all on your own."

"Yeah, and you did such a fantastic job of helping me when I made mistakes."

"I did plenty," her mom retorted.

"Oh, really?" Rage bubbled up in Lia's chest. She should've known this would be how the night would end. It didn't even matter anymore that they were easily within hearing range of everyone in the banquet hall. Anger covered up everything else, obliterating any self-control Lia had left. *Fine, then.* They would do this here.

Chapter Twelve

"Grandmamma was there for me when all you did was cry and moan about how much I'd disappointed this family," said Lia, crossing her arms. "So don't act like you sacrificed anything at all for me."

"I raised you. I did everything I could to help you succeed, even when you did idiotic things like get kicked out of every school we ever sent you to."

"Don't act like you were there for me, Mom. Just don't. No one buys your little act."

"You're the most ungrateful, spoiled child. My mother has done nothing but damage you and make it so you can't do anything on your own."

"Grandmamma was the one who came and got me in New Mexico, Mom, not you. I wouldn't call that spoiling me. I was stuck in that place for over two weeks until Grandmamma stepped in."

The pain was still fresh. The girl that Lia had gotten into a fight with in England had a family who'd pressed charges. A private security team had held Lia for almost a day before taking her back to a juvenile facility in New Mexico. But that wasn't the worst part.

"I was going through a very difficult time then, Ophelia."

"Please! You were in Bermuda."

"I went there for relaxation. I was struggling," said Sonia piously. "I've gone through difficulties you couldn't possibly imagine."

"You were starving for attention, like you always are. And when they called to tell you what had happened, you told them you weren't coming to get me," said Lia, her voice catching in her throat. "You told them to keep me there, that the structure might teach me a lesson."

Sonia broke her gaze with Lia, and for a moment there was silence, broken only by the murmur of voices behind them from the crowd in the banquet room. Finally, Sonia tossed her head and shrugged one elegant shoulder with a coldness that shocked even Lia, who didn't think it was possible to be shocked by anything her mother did anymore.

"You needed to be taught a lesson," Sonia sneered. "You're so smug, being your grandmother's favorite."

"What is wrong with you?" said Lia. "How could you say that about me? That place was horrible. I was stuck there until Grandmamma got there and got me out. You just left me in there."

"Don't be so dramatic."

"You have no idea what that was like, or what that did to me. But you don't care. You don't care about anyone except yourself. Is that why you came here tonight? To harass the headmistress about—about my tuition money?"

"I just asked your headmistress if you could be placed on scholarship, and she said no. Your two years here have been paid in full. I think that with the generous donation made from this family that exceptions could be made, but it looks like they want to be stubborn about it."

"Why in the world would I be placed on scholarship if my tuition is paid for?"

"Because your grandmother has cut me off completely," Sonia whined, her voice panicked. "I have nothing. She spends all her money on you, and this school, and anything else you need. What about me? What about what I need?"

"You seriously thought the school would place me on scholarship so that you could have my tuition money back? There are girls who actually need financial aid, Sonia. I'm not one of them."

"Thanks to your grandmother, who thinks it's important to keep you in satin and pearls while I go without."

Lia just shook her head. Her entire body was

vibrating with anger. This wasn't the first time that her grandmother had cut Sonia off, if that was what was really happening. Lia had seen it over and over—her mom would blow through hundreds of thousands of dollars on clothes and whatever else, and her grandmother would cut her off. It was pathetic, and Lia felt disgusted as she stared at the delusional woman in front of her.

"Get a job, Mom. Stop harassing the people in my life. Stay away from Grandmamma, and stay away from me."

Lia turned and started to walk away, her boots echoing on the floor. Sonia scurried after her as she headed down a hallway, clutching at her arm.

"Lia, wait. Please."

"What do you want from me?"

"You can talk to her for me. You can get her to change her mind," Sonia wheedled.

"Why would I do anything to help you?"

This hurt, too—the way her mom only cared about her when she needed something.

"I'm your mother, Ophelia. I'm your mother," she repeated. "And I'm your guardian. I can make sure that you don't go abroad with Lenore this summer, or maybe that the terms of your trust fund are changed."

Lia doubted that was within her mom's power, but she still went cold as she turned to face her mother. "Grandmamma would never let that happen."

"I could fight her on it. You're my child, not hers, and as long as you're a minor I have control over you. I can forbid you to see her, to have contact with her at all."

"This is how you're going to convince me to talk to Grandmamma for you? By threatening me? You have lost your mind," said Lia. "Look, Mom, go home. You sound insane."

"Agree to talk to her for me."

"No. I won't do it. You're an adult, and I don't owe you anything. You need to handle your own problems."

"You're going to regret this," said Sonia. "You ungrateful little traitor."

"Shut up, Mom."

The two of them stood there in the hallway, tears running down Lia's face that she barely noticed. She wasn't sad, she was just angry at the way this happened over and over, angry at the fact that she had a mother who tried to coerce her into conning her grandmother out of money, a mother who had never cared about who Lia was as a person. Sonia tossed her hair back and adjusted the purse on her shoulder. Lia noticed her mother's eyes already held that unnatural shininess that she developed when she was in her hysterical mood.

"You have no right to talk to me this way," Sonia said.

"You're going to try for dignified, now? Really? You just begged me to ask Grandmamma for money for you. You're pathetic."

"You'll show respect when you speak to me. Like it or not, Lia, we're family, and family takes care of each other."

"You're no family of mine," whispered Lia. "I wish

you would leave and never, ever speak to me again. I mean it. Get out."

"Lia—

"Get out!" Lia shrieked, and Sonia smiled a twisted, vicious smile.

"This isn't over," she said, pointing a manicured finger at Lia. Then she turned on her heels and walked away. Lia watched her go down the hallway, listening to the sound of her footsteps fading into the silence. The front door opened, and then Lia heard it slam closed. Wiping away tears, Lia whirled and ran down the hallway.

As she turned corners and headed back to her room, Lia's chest was tight with shock and rage. *Why, of all days, did this have to be the day Mom pulled something like this?*

I should've known, thought Lia bitterly. *I should have known she didn't just feel like visiting me. She's never done anything in her life unless there was some-thing in it for her. Oh, God, why did I say she could come? Why did I have to think this time might actually be different?*

But she knew why. She always hoped that one day her mom would come through for her, that the two of them could start over and be friends.

I'm an idiot, thought Lia. *I listened to Dr. Lowenstein, who said it would be a good idea, even when I knew better. I'm so, so stupid.*

Finally, she got to her room and threw open the door. The place was blissfully dark and quiet—Darlene must be at the library again. Lia went straight to her bedroom and slammed the door behind her, leaning her back against the smooth wood. Lifting her hands to her forehead, Lia started to cry—huge, choking sobs—as she slid down the door and wrapped her arms around her knees, hugging herself tight.

Chapter Thirteen

For a long time, Lia stayed that way, curled in a ball at the foot of her bedroom door. Eventually, she stopped crying, and just sat there, toying with a piece of her hair absently. Her anger had faded to numbness; she was exhausted, though, deep down in her bones. This day had been a complete disaster. The things her mother had said to her were nasty, even by Sonia's standard. This thing going on with her grandmother must be a big deal. To ask the headmistress for Lia's tuition money back . . . Lia shook her head. That was really a new low. Did she really think the headmistress would agree to that? Maybe she had honestly thought it was possible. Lia had known her mother since birth and she still didn't understand how her mind worked. She was completely delusional.

Lia laid her head down on her knees, her mom's words replaying in her head. More than anything, Lia wished that she were eighteen. This was the last straw. She couldn't stand being under the control of her mother anymore. And she had more than a year to wait. It seemed like an eternity, an eternity stuck being connected to the woman who had left Lia to rot in a juvenile detention facility.

As much as Lia hated thinking about it, the memories roared up in a never-ending flood. The smell of the antiseptic, and the scratchiness of the uniform they'd forced her to wear. The other girls had hated Lia on sight, had terrified her at night by waking her out of a dead sleep or simply walking by her bed over and over again in the dark, their footsteps muffled. The lights were fluorescent and flickering and they gave Lia a constant headache, but the worst part was how completely alone she felt. It had taken days for her grandmother to straighten out the charges and get Lia a court date so she could be released. Lia hadn't cried, not a single tear, until she came into the courtroom that day and saw her grandmother sitting there, and then she lost it. She'd sobbed throughout the entire hearing, even though they said she'd be released into the custody of family since the charges against her had been dropped thanks to her grandmother. Deep down, Lia knew that it was her fault she'd wound up in there—but to have a mother who had known she was there and simply didn't care was the most painful betrayal of all. Being stuck in that place, even for a short time, had changed her. There was no going back to the person she was before, not that Sonia would care.

Lia finally sighed and stood up slowly from her place on the carpet. She wanted a shower, and then all she wanted to do was go to sleep and forget this ever happened. Sighing, Lia took off each of her earrings and her necklace and laid them on top of her dresser and turned on the hot water, but even the soothing jets didn't improve her mood. Lia pulled on her oldest flannel pajamas after she toweled off and crawled right under the covers, pulling them up and over her head. Then she lay awake for a long time, tossing and turning, before she finally drifted off.

The next day, Lia spent nearly the entire day in the library trying to study. She called her grandmother several times, but she hadn't answered yet. Of course this would be the time she was out of the country and unavailable. Lia sat in the library tapping her pens against her notebook, music blasting in her ears, and tried to focus. Her mom's words kept repeating in her head, over and over, like a song on repeat that she couldn't turn off. Girls came and went as the day passed, some on their own, but more in groups, and Lia was more isolated than ever. Every single person seemed to be staring at her, or whispering about her behind their hands. Honestly, Lia couldn't blame them in this case. She and Sonia had been right outside the banquet room, and they hadn't been quiet. Even with the crowd of people making small talk inside that room, there's no way they hadn't been heard. The knowledge did nothing to improve Lia's mood.

Dinner was Lia's favorite, garlic and herb-crusted prime rib, but she barely ate. Then she tried her grandmother again with no success before going to bed early. This weekend couldn't end quickly enough. For the first time in probably her entire life, she was looking forward to Monday. At the very least, classes the next day would be a distraction.

Lia got to the photo lab early, as usual, on Monday afternoon. Entering the classroom was like entering a sanctuary. Breathing her first sigh of genuine relief since Saturday, Lia settled into her station in the darkroom and began sifting through her images. There were a few that she wanted to put into the developing trays; now, more than ever, she was determined to find something perfect for the exhibition. She loved macro images, and Lia had taken several extreme close-ups of day-to-day things, like a grapefruit and her own eyelashes, and they'd turned out beautifully in black and white. Her work was always just a little different than everyone else's. And if her submissions were exceptional, the scouts for art schools would remember her when she started applying to colleges next fall. At this point, anything that would get her into an art school that was somewhere away from her mother was an option. She could even go abroad, potentially—Grandmamma would love that.

Lia heard the rest of the class come in from her place inside the darkroom, but she stayed where she was in the quiet room full of soft red light. The teacher usually didn't mind when she didn't come out for the introduction of class, as long as she was working on a project. After a couple of her prints were finished rinsing clean in the running water of the sink, Lia grabbed them with the tongs and held them carefully by the edges. She pushed the revolving door of the darkroom open so she could look at her prints in the light. Frowning, Lia studied the photos in the light of the classroom. Her new favorite photo was one of her own hair in the wind, taken with the camera's self-timer and a tripod. It was stark, and visually arresting, almost bleak—nothing but the wild blowing of her hair, with moody clouds in the background. It was good, and the rest of her photos, including the close-ups, were good too, but something was still missing. *Should I use a filter or something?*

Lia went to her seat at one of the long tables and continued to study her photos, opening the drawer next to her where she kept more developed prints of hers so she could compare her work. Dimly, she became aware of the sound of semi-hushed voices coming from farther down the table. Grace was sitting in a group of girls who were all darting glances at Lia, giggles erupting every few seconds. Lia just rolled her eyes and ignored them. She knew what they were discussing, and while she wished they'd mind their own business—it would be a while before what had happened at Parents' Weekend died down. Then she heard Grace's voice, rising in volume so she could clearly make out every word.

"Her mom is totally insane. I mean, I don't know what that woman was thinking. I think that's why Ophelia is so weird—her mother is a whack job."

Lia tried to picture a calm sea, but all she could picture were her hands around Grace's throat.

"All those rumors about her family must not be true," Grace continued. "They seem like trash to me, definitely not anything like royalty. She's been fooling all of us, the little liar."

That's it.

"Hey, Grace," said Lia sweetly, standing up from her stool. She sauntered over to where Grace was sitting with her groupies, several of whose mouths dropped open as Lia approached. "I have an idea. How about you keep your stupid mouth shut?"

Grace darted a glance left and right, but Lia hadn't

spoken loudly. The teacher sat obliviously at her desk, grading projects with swipes of her red pen.

"I don't think you're in any position to be giving orders," said Grace, smirking. "Not after what happened this weekend."

"I'm pretty sure the same thing happens at your house every weekend, Grace, so what do you care? Isn't that what life is like for someone as gross as you? Except your mom probably wouldn't have been wearing designer shoes while she screamed at you, I can pretty much bet on that."

One of Grace's groupies buried a nervous giggle in her hand. The rest of the group gawked, their stares switching from Grace to Lia and back again. Grace's face had gone dark with rage.

"Don't say a word against my family," said Grace.

"Why not? You certainly like to talk about mine."

Grace's eyes nearly bulged from her head; she stepped toward Lia and then glanced at the teacher and stepped back again, thinking better of it.

"You shut your mouth," hissed Grace. "Or you'll regret it."

"I really don't think I will."

She turned to walk away, leaving Grace standing there livid with her fists clench.

"At least my mother cares about me," she said to Lia's back. "Yours clearly doesn't. You're nothing to her at all."

For once, Lia was at a loss for words. The rage bubbled up inside her again, and she turned back to face Grace. Lia could barely see her through the haze of red that clouded her vision, and her fists balled in at her sides.

"You're the one who is nothing, Grace, not me," said Lia, slowly and clearly. "And I promise you, you will regret saying that."

It took all her willpower for Lia to walk back to her seat and sit down on her stool. Now wasn't the time to punish Grace—no. That would come later. She'd gone too far this time. Lia would plan something very special for her. She was done playing nice.

Chapter Fourteen

A few hours later, Lia hesitated at the door of her appointment with Dr. Lowenstein. For the first time in a long time, she felt apprehensive about meeting with him. So much had happened that she wasn't even sure she wanted to work through. There was still so much anger inside her directed toward her mother. Blowing out a breath, Lia knocked on the door and entered.

Dr. Lowenstein rose from his usual chair to greet her, and Lia's heart twisted at his smile. It was just such a comparison between his reaction to seeing her, and her mother's. This was one of the few people whom Lia felt actually cared about her.

"Hello, Lia," he said as she sat down. "How was your weekend?"

Lia didn't know what to say. She hesitated, picking at a thread on her chair.

"It was pretty awful," she admitted. "It was terrible, actually. My mom and I got in the biggest fight of my life, which is really saying something, with our track record."

"Oh, Lia." Dr. Lowenstein's face was pained. "I'm so sorry to hear that. What happened?"

"I don't want to go into the details," said Lia, shaking her head. "But it sucked. And the worst part is that I had a bad feeling about the entire weekend. I know my mom like the back of my hand, and something didn't feel right. But I listened to you, and I tried to be nice, and look what happened. The exact same thing that always happens whenever we are in the same room for more than thirty seconds."

"Lia, I didn't mean to—"

"No, just don't."

Lia sprang up from her chair. She hated having to relive the weekend all over again, and she was still boiling from the altercation with Grace earlier. It was too much to face Dr. Lowenstein's pity on top of everything else.

"Lia, you don't have to talk about anything that you don't want to. But if you want to work through what happened this weekend and get rid of some of that anger, I think that would be a good idea."

"Yeah, well, you also thought inviting my mother would be a good idea, and look how far that got me," Lia shot back. For a moment the room was silent, ripe with tension. Suddenly, Lia felt like she couldn't breathe.

"Look, I need to go," she said, grabbing her backpack again. "I can't do this today. I don't want to talk about anything. I just want to be alone."

Before Dr. Lowenstein could protest, Lia was out the door, trying to forget the hurt look on his face.

Her chest felt like it was going to explode. She needed to get out of here.

Lia walked briskly back to her room, her feet leading her across the grounds. She was panting by the time she got to her suite. Letting herself in, Lia dropped her shoulder bag on the floor and immediately went to her room to get her easel. She dragged it into the common room, laid down sheets of plastic, and changed into her painting clothes. Tying her hair up into a ponytail, Lia mixed a palette of dark colors, with a few jewel tones for accents, and studied the fresh white paper on the easel. The paintbrush swirled two colors together, and Lia got started with a bold swipe across the canvas. There was no room for thinking when she was painting. All she could do was let the idea in her mind expand, brushstroke by brushstroke, going by instinct alone. As she painted, Lia tried to breathe deeply and center her mind, but her anger refused to completely fade. Halfway through the painting, Lia swore and tore the sheet down again, crumpling it. *Why could nothing go right today?*

As Lia stood with her hands on her hips, studying her new sheet of paper and waiting for inspiration to hit, her cell phone began to buzz on the coffee table. She grabbed it absently, putting the device to her ear without checking to see who was calling.

"Hello?"

"Lia?"

Lia smiled, her heart fluttering in her chest. "Well, hi, stranger."

"Oh, Lia, dear, it's good to hear your voice. Can you hear me alright? I'm not sure if these transcontinental calls come through clearly."

"I can hear you just fine, Grandmamma."

Lia sat down on the couch, smiling even though she couldn't see Lenore's face.

"Well, I'm glad to finally speak with you. I'm sorry it's been strictly email lately—even with all the new contraptions out these days, the reception at our estate is sketchy at best. I'm staying in Paris tonight, so I'm calling from the hotel."

Lenore's voice was clipped, precise, and imperious in tone—it was a voice that was used to people jumping when she spoke an order. It warmed only when talking to her granddaughter.

"Oh, you're in Paris now?" asked Lia.

"I certainly am. I fly back to the States tomorrow night. It was the earliest flight that I could get back, since the jet is also being repaired and I have to fly commercial. Incompetent fools."

"The earliest one? Why the rush? And why are you calling so late—I love it, don't get me wrong, but isn't it super late in your time zone?"

There was a brief pause. Lia frowned, then looked at her phone, wondering if the call had been dropped.

"Yes, it is late, but I needed to speak with you anyhow, Lia. I had a call from your mother yesterday."

"Oh, man." Lia rubbed a hand over her eyes. She was so tired of talking about this. "So, she must have filled you in on what happened, then, right? It was quite a scene, but it's going to be okay, Grandmamma. She was just in one of her psychotic moods. Did you cut her off again, though, or was she making that up?"

"I certainly did," sighed Lenore. "After she'd squandered more than you can imagine in the course of a month. I hate to speak ill of family, but your mother is a tornado, and she's growing more and more erratic as time goes on. She's dreadfully spoiled; why, she throws tantrums like a child."

"She calls me spoiled," said Lia, smiling wryly. "That's the pot calling the kettle black."

"Yes, it is. Lia, your mother was in quite a state when she finally got hold of me. She made a lot of ridiculous accusations and essentially ranted for twenty minutes in my ear. I thought nothing of it, except to make a note to check that you were alright. But my lawyer contacted me this morning, Lia, and your mother has unfortunately gone through with at least some of her threats." Lenore's voice was frosty now. Lia could hear the layers of anger hidden in her voice.

"What do you mean?"

"I mean that it looks like she is actually pursuing an order of restraint against me. She doesn't want me to see you, or contact you. She also doesn't want me taking you abroad this summer, though how that affects her I really have no idea."

Lia's fingertips had gone completely numb.

"You can't be serious," she said. "She can't do this."

"I'm afraid that as your mother she can definitely push for a restraining order. I should be able to throw it out soon, as the grounds for it simply don't exist—but until then, Lia, I need you not to contact me."

Lia's eyes filled with tears, and she shook her head slowly from side to side.

"What? No. I can't."

"Lia, darling, it's only temporary. That I promise you. As soon as I get myself home I will get this entire situation straightened out. My lawyers trump your mother's any day of the week, and she knows that. She just wants to make a splash, and to pay me back for cutting her off financially. I tell you, Lia, this is the last straw. Of all the things your mother has ever done, trying to keep me from you is the cruelest." Her voice darkened, and Lia knew that her mom didn't stand a chance against Lenore. But how long would it take to get the order thrown out? Her grandmother was the only person in the world who truly loved her. Without her, she would be completely alone, and even if it was only a brief period of time, that was terrifying.

"There's nothing you can do now?" Lia asked.

"We'll see when I'm back in the States. I promise, this will be resolved as quickly as possible, Lia. But until then, no calls, and no emails, alright? I'll reach out to you again once everything is settled."

"Okay," Lia whispered. It was stupid to feel abandoned. It was only temporary.

"Okay, darling. I'll talk to you soon. I love you."

"I love you, too," said Lia, and the line went dead.

Lia sat in her empty suite, listening to the silence. Never had she hated her mother more than she did now; who did she think she was? Lia covered her face in her hands, her chest tight with pain. Taking a deep breath, Lia changed out of her painting clothes and tried to cheer up by reminding herself they were serving chocolate chip cookies for dessert tonight.

Don't even think about crying, Lia told herself. *It isn't worth it.*

Lia sat at one of the tables in the dining hall by herself with her headphones in. She was nibbling on a cookie, but even that wasn't improving her mood. Even though she ate almost every night alone, tonight she felt especially lonely. There was a big difference between being lonely and being alone, and tonight Lia felt the difference keenly. She stood up to clear her tray, and as she turned around, Grace came out of nowhere and bumped her shoulder deliberately into

Lia's. Grace's chocolate pudding flew into the air and splattered on the floor, covering Lia's shoes and half her face as Grace jumped free.

"What is wrong with you?" said Lia, wiping pudding furiously out of her eyes. "You did that on purpose." There was even pudding on the front of her shirt. Grace smirked, her eyes disdainful. Lia glanced behind her and realized the entire dining hall was staring at the two of them, and worse, some of them were laughing. Lia looked down at her pudding-covered self and back up into Grace's smirking eyes and something in her snapped. It had been too long since she'd stood up for herself, too long since she reminded everyone, especially Grace, who they were dealing with. Lia resisted doing something here and now. This wasn't the place, where everyone was watching. Instead, she smirked back at Grace and walked away.

"That's it? You're not going to say anything?" said Grace as Lia walked toward the door.

"No. I'm not going to say anything at all." The

door shut behind her, and Lia's mind jumped into motion. This was what she did best: revenge.

Chapter Fifteen

For more than a week, Lia lay low. She didn't make waves, and she tried not to do anything out of the ordinary. The trick was to wait a little while, lull everyone into a state of total complacency, and then do something they never saw coming. Now she just had to plan exactly how she was going to get back at Grace for being an enormous pain for so long. There were so many possibilities, but she had to choose the perfect one. Lia was riding the edge of her own anger: anger at her mother, at Grace, at everything in her life that was wrong. She didn't want to think about any of the things that were going on in her life, like whether she'd ever be able to talk to her grandmother again, or the stupid project for the exhibition that she couldn't manage to get right. So far, she hadn't heard anything new from her grandmother or Sonia, and waiting was agony. Thoughts of how she would get revenge on Grace were a welcome distraction. It didn't have to be anything too insane, just something petty enough to cause her some grief. But it had to be untraceable, with no way of connecting it to Lia. She would make sure of that. Then, just when she felt she'd scraped the bottom of the barrel in regards to good ideas, an opportunity fell right into her lap.

One morning in the middle of the week, Lia's photography and design teacher announced that there would be a mandatory presentation the next day, since they would have a guest speaker attending class to talk about the Advanced Placement exam. Lia eyed Grace from across the room as a plan formed in her mind. This could work for her. All she needed to do was to go to Nurse Lori and complain of a few specific symptoms, and she'd be in business. The deep and constant burn of anger in her chest was familiar, and anger was easier to handle than sadness. This would just be one innocent little prank. No one would know it was her who had put it together. She would be safe, and for all intents and purposes, she'd look innocent as an angel, even though she was anything but.

Lia woke up that Thursday with more energy than she had had in days. Today, her plan would fall into place. Jumping out of bed, Lia got dressed in her uniform and went straight to the dining hall to have an early breakfast. In her pocket was a small bottle, a bottle that she was going to use to make Grace reconsider messing with Ophelia Koroleva. It would all happen this afternoon. Every afternoon during their class, Grace drank tea from a metal thermos. Lia had seen it a million times. It was silver and it had her initials monogrammed on the side, which

Lia found idiotic. She was going to use that thermos to her advantage.

Lia fidgeted through the first half of her day; luckily, she didn't have any tests to worry about, but she still found it hard to concentrate. This was the hardest part: the anticipation. Once it was over, she would be totally relaxed. Lia skipped lunch and went straight to her photography and design classroom and spent the hour working on developing more of her own prints—and making sure Grace's thermos was in her locker where it was typically kept. When Lia cracked it open to double check, it was right where it should be. That was step one.

The class filed in as the bell rang, and Lia watched Grace grab her thermos from her locker and fill it with hot water for her tea, chatting with her friends as she did so. Grace set it on the long table behind her as she turned the other way on her stool in the direction of the presenter. Lia stood up from where she'd been sitting quietly with her notebook, and casually walked around the back of the room. As she passed the area where Grace was sitting, the teacher turned the lights off for the presentation. At that exact moment, Lia reached out and squeezed the contents of the little bottle soundlessly into Grace's tea. It was all over in less than four seconds, and Lia was back in her seat in less than ten. No one had noticed. She was sure of it.

"Okay, class, please give a warm round of applause to our guest speaker for the day. And keep in mind this presentation when you begin making your own choices for your portfolios."

Lia clapped politely, and she eyed Grace. Grace reached back for her tea and took a healthy swallow, and Lia had to stifle a smile. Now, all she had to do was wait. Lia tried to listen to what the speaker was saying, and take notes from her slideshow, but the woman had a droning voice and it was all Lia could do to not stare directly at Grace. Out of the corner of her eye, she watched Grace gulp down the entire thermos of tea in the first twenty minutes, and then she had to bite her lip to keep from grinning. Forcing herself to keep a straight face, Lia chewed on her pen and made herself look forward. She didn't want to look too obvious.

Another ten minutes passed, and then Lia noticed Grace fidgeting in her seat. Her friends began to wrinkle their noses and scoot their stools away from her, and Lia wanted to laugh out loud. The look on Grace's face changed slowly from casual interest in the lecture to mild concern. Lia saw her lean forward slightly, rubbing a hand across her tummy. Her expression contorted, and then a look of abject horror filled her eyes. This was the part Lia liked best. There were audible noises coming from Grace's stomach now, and the rumbling was starting to become distracting. The teacher, standing in the front corner of the room, looked in Grace's direction and glared. Lia blinked her eyes innocently, and jotted down a few notes from the slideshow, as though she were the only one in the room who didn't notice anything but the presentation.

Grace was in visible discomfort at this point. Her

stomach had expanded like a balloon, with her buttons straining at their seams as air filled her gut. She was hunched forward miserably with an expression of genuine terror that delighted Lia. Her stomach grumbled again, and Grace's friends shifted as far away from her as they could get. The entire classroom was murmuring quietly, with girls glancing at Grace and then shrugging to their neighbors. It was clear something was wrong, but what? Lia knew that Grace was fighting the feelings in her body, hoping it was a bout of stomach pain from lunch that would subside, or at least be manageable until after class. But she was fighting a losing battle, and Lia knew it was a manner of minutes before she would crack.

Finally, that moment came. Grace leaped from her stool, her hands on her stomach, and ran to where the teacher stood at the front of the room. This professor in particular was especially strict about students leaving the room during presentations; she had a deep, abiding hatred for cell phones and was strict on bathroom breaks just because she didn't want girls to pull out the dreaded devices. The entire class was looking at Grace now, who was deep in earnest conversation with the teacher. Key words carried even all the way to where Lia was, and the teacher shook her head at Grace's request. Lia nearly laughed out loud—this was going better than she could have hoped for. Grace pleaded, but the teacher stood firm, and Grace was forced to go back to her stool, climbing on again gingerly.

She only lasted another forty-five seconds, practically writhing in pain, before she jumped up from the stool, clapped her hands firmly on the seat of her skirt, and ran from the room. As she ran, the sound of more violent gurgles from her stomach followed her out, and laughter erupted from the room. By the time she reached the hallway and the door slammed shut behind her, Lia knew Grace had left it too long. The laxatives had had too much time to take effect. Now, she would be known as the girl who had an upset tummy, a *very* upset tummy, in the middle of class. The presenter had to deal with girls whispering and outbursts of laughter for the rest of the class period, and Lia knew she'd succeeded. All around the room, girls were either gossiping about what had happened, or subtly texting their friends in other class periods, avoiding the teacher's eagle eye for cell phones. By the time class was dismissed, Lia heard the story exaggerate further and further, growing more disgusting with each embellishment. Grace was the talk of the school, and Lia practically skipped to her next class.

Dr. Lowenstein had emailed Lia the day before and sent his regrets, but he'd had to cancel their usual session to handle a family emergency. Lia couldn't help but feel a little relieved. She didn't think she was ready to face him in another session just yet. He had a way of looking through her, right to her core, and Lia wasn't ready to deal with that now. Plus, he had a way of calming her down and forcing her to think rationally, and that wasn't what she wanted, either. He probably would have made her feel guilty about giving Grace the laxatives and embarrassing her in front of the whole school, and Lia wanted to be wicked just a little while longer. It felt so good to stop fighting for control over her anger, and to just make decisions based on impulse. Lia was playing a dangerous little game, but she loved the thrill.

All the talk Lia heard in the hallway on the way to dinner that night was about Grace and her little accident, and that delighted her. The story was gaining even more notoriety than she'd expected, and not a single person suspected her of anything. It was a perfectly executed prank, humiliating and effective. Grace didn't reappear that night, though Lia kept a watchful eye out for her in the dining hall as she treated herself to another creamy cheesecake bar with graham cracker and butter crust. It was likely that she'd be in the restroom for the rest of the night. Lia had only pulled off that prank once before, and it wasn't even close to an entire bottle. She would be surprised if Grace was well enough to attend class the next day. The thought made her practically giddy with a dark, smug happiness. Mission *definitely* accomplished.

Chapter Sixteen

The next morning, Lia went into the dining hall for breakfast and still didn't see Grace. *She must still be recovering,* thought Lia, *or hiding.* But if she was hiding to avoid the gossip, it wasn't going to work. Lia knew that much from experience. Girls were going to talk about you regardless, whether or not you showed your face after something like that. Lia finished off her third croissant and grabbed her shoulder bag to head to class, thoughts of Grace leaving her mind. Instead, she continued considering her piece for the art exhibition.

It was coming up soon, in just a few weeks, and

most students who were submitting a piece had already been working on it since the beginning of the year. No one was as far behind as Lia. She had the bunch of black and white photos she'd printed, and some smaller paintings that she could potentially flesh out to create something, but nothing she'd been working on continuously. The paintings were from earlier in the year—one a bold splash of color, a beach sunset, and the other a stark, gloomy landscape pulled from her own memory of the English countryside. Both were good, exceptional even—but Lia wanted something absolutely perfect. The landscapes were lovely, but not quite personal enough, somehow.

Lia tapped a pencil on her notebook in Algebra II and formed ideas in her mind, her fingers itching for something to create. She'd done a couple charcoal sketches of her own eyes on canvas earlier in the year—those pieces were also a possibility. Adding to them might be an option. Closing her eyes, Lia pictured her sketches, then her paintings, and then the photos, trying to mentally choose which were the strongest. When class ended, she got out of her chair and headed to the dining hall. She'd have to scarf down lunch and then go right to the lab to keep working. Today was the day the chefs were doing each meal Italian-themed, though. There would be gourmet pasta, eighteen different kinds of wood-fired pizza, green salads, and more varieties of cheese than Lia had known existed. Lia's mouth watered. *Okay, stay long enough to try the chicken pesto and the Gorgonzola cheese pizzas, and then get to work,* Lia told herself sternly as she waited in line. Her stomach growled.

Lia wound up getting to her photography and design class just as the bell rang, and then she was forced to take a seat with everyone else as the teacher introduced the class. Out of the corner of her eye, Lia saw Grace emerge from the darkroom and skulk to her seat, glaring daggers at Lia. Lia thought she looked a little pale, but otherwise normal—she'd obviously recovered since her ordeal yesterday. Grace turned on her stool to face Lia, still glaring, and Lia waggled her fingers at her in an ironic wave.

"Alright, ladies, go ahead and begin working on your projects. The darkroom is open, and I'll be at my desk if anyone needs anything," the teacher finished. Lia hopped off her stool and headed to the back of the room where she'd stashed her older projects, like a few of her charcoal sketches and the watercolor paintings. Lia sifted through the pages and canvasses piled on the back table, but she couldn't find any pieces of her own. Lia frowned, trying to remember if she'd moved them or something. As far as she could recall, she'd set them right here after they'd been graded. *Where is all my stuff?*

Lia went to her locker at the other end of the studio, but it was mostly empty except for paper scraps and test strips from developing her film. There were a few bad negatives, left over from a poorly developed roll of film, but nothing else. Maybe she'd misremembered and left her older work in the darkroom somewhere. It was possible that she'd stacked everything next to one of the enlargers and just forgotten about it. Lia made her way to the darkroom's revolving door and pushed her way inside.

It took a moment for her eyes to adjust to the red lighting, and then she moved over to where the enlargers were sitting in a sectioned-off row. Her feet seemed to be sliding on something—had someone dropped a print on the floor? The ground needed to be clear in the darkroom at all times because of the poor lighting. Lia kneeled down, peering at the floor. It was covered in pieces of what looked like paper, and Lia saw the scraps covered the ground of nearly the entire darkroom. She stood up slowly, handfuls of the scraps in her hands. Those were her pictures. She recognized her images in some of the larger chunks—a scrap of her grapefruit photo, and another of her countryside painting. And over there, in the corner, didn't that pile look like the photo of her hair in the wind, and the sunset watercolor?

Lia's heart was in her throat. She stumbled around the darkroom, grabbing pieces of whatever she could find on the floor. Her charcoal sketches, her black and white photos, the paintings inspired by her night-time dreams—they were all gone, cut into little tiny pieces. Lia's eyes burned with furious, unshed tears. There were more scraps covering the tables, and even some scattered over the developing area. Everything she'd worked on all year, every piece she'd created, and all her options for the exhibition . . . they were all destroyed. Lia's chest heaved as she stood alone in the darkroom, fighting for breath, her hands full of the tiny pieces of everything she'd been working on. *Who would do this?* But even as the thought entered her mind, she knew the answer. There was only one person here who hated her enough to do this. For the briefest of moments, Lia fought to stay calm, and then her willpower evaporated and was replaced only by blind fury. There were no more thoughts in her head—there was nothing but anger and the need to see it justified.

Lia turned on her heels and shoved her way back through the revolving door, knocking several girls out of the way as she went. Her hatred had completely obliterated everything else; her common sense, her self-control—all of it was gone. She'd been pushed too far. Lia strode into the classroom and went straight for Grace. A few large steps brought her to where Grace was sitting on her stool, and in one smooth motion, Lia stepped directly into her line of vision.

"You destroyed it all! Everything that I've been working on all year!"

"What is wrong with you, Ophelia?" shrieked Grace, shoving her hair out of her face.

"I know it was you, Grace. All my drawings, paintings—they're all destroyed, and I know you did it!"

As the girls continued to scream at each other, Lia reached toward Grace in a blind rage, but the teacher was between them in another second. Then she was scolding them both, holding the two girls forcefully apart, and the buzzing in Lia's head prevented her from hearing anything but the incessant, violent pounding of her own heartbeat.

Chapter Seventeen

The girls were marched out of the classroom immediately, Lia's irate photography teacher with a hand on each of their shoulders.

"In all my years here, I have never seen such behavior," she spluttered. "You two are going straight to the headmistress, this very instant."

"Why do I have to go?" Grace asked as they walked across campus. "I didn't do anything! It was all Ophelia. She's insane."

"Quiet!" shouted the teacher. "And you were implicit as well, Grace."

"This is stupid," said Lia, speaking for the first

time since the fight. "Grace started this, and she knows it."

Grace lunged for her, grasping fruitlessly, and the teacher shoved them apart again, shaking her head. She continued muttering angrily to herself as she marched Lia and Grace straight to the door of the headmistress's office. Lia's adrenaline rush was fading, and she was still angry, but sick fear was beginning to take hold as her common sense reasserted itself. *What have I done?* The teacher knocked on the huge double doors, and the headmistress's voice rang out from inside.

"You may enter."

The doors opened, and the girls walked inside. Lia took a seat at one of the two chairs that sat in front of the headmistress's enormous oak desk. Headmistress Chambers removed her glasses, folding her hands on a stack of papers.

As the teacher launched into an explanation of the afternoon's events, Lia folded her arms and sat sullenly. The headmistress's face never changed. She listened calmly, her gaze flicking from Lia to Grace and back again.

"I just pulled them off each other," the teacher huffed. "They were acting like a couple of wild animals, screaming, and Lia lunged at Grace. It was disgraceful."

"Thank you, Miss Rosa," said the headmistress smoothly. "You did the right thing by bringing them in. I can handle it from here."

The teacher shot a last furious look in the girls' direction and then sniffed, turned on her heel, and left the room.

Now, it was just the two girls with Headmistress Chambers, and for a few seconds there was only silence.

"This is all Ophelia's fault," Grace blurted out. "She came at me first."

"I heard, Grace," Headmistress Chambers responded.

"She's crazy. She did it for no reason. She just ran out of the darkroom and practically tackled me."

"I did not tackle you!" Lia protested. "And you know why I was yelling," she continued, glaring at Grace. "Don't play dumb."

Grace sneered at her. "Well, maybe you shouldn't have pulled that little prank on me yesterday."

"I don't know what you're talking about."

"What prank?" the headmistress asked, and Grace reddened.

"I think that she—I mean, I don't know, but . . . I think she fed me laxatives somehow. I'm still not sure how, exactly, but I know it was her."

For a moment, Lia could've sworn the headmistress's lips twitched.

"Do you have any proof, Grace?"

Grace squirmed in her chair. "No, ma'am, not right now."

"Alright, then. Lia, why did you begin the altercation with Grace?"

"She destroyed all of my art projects," Lia said quietly. "Everything I've been working on all year. It's all gone."

"Grace, is this true?"

"I don't know anything about that."

Grace wasn't nearly as good of a liar as Lia was. Her face turned bright red and she cowered beneath the headmistress's stare.

"Are you certain of that, Grace?" Lia watched Grace struggle to defend herself and was thankful that although Grace should have plenty of experience lying, given what she was involved in, she didn't quite have the brain cells to think quickly on her feet. Pity.

"Okay, I might know something about it," Grace stammered. "Look, it wasn't just me. My friends helped. I just wanted to get back at Lia for the prank."

"I see," said the headmistress. "So, you admit to destroying her projects intentionally?"

"I, well . . . yeah, okay, fine."

"I thank you for your honesty, Grace," said the headmistress. "You may go."

"I can go?"

"Yes. We'll discuss your punishment later."

"Wait, I'm being punished? That's not fair. You heard the teacher. Ophelia came at me first. And she poisoned me!"

"That's enough pointing of fingers, Grace. I'll be in touch with you later."

Grace stood up to leave. She glared at Lia as she left, and then it was just the headmistress and Lia in the room.

"Well, Miss Koroleva," said the headmistress. "I have to say I really hoped not to see you in this room."

Lia folded her arms and sat silently. If she was going to be expelled, what was the point of arguing, anyway?

"Behavior like you exhibited earlier is not tolerated at this school, Lia. Not under any circumstances, provoked or unprovoked."

"I'm sorry," said Lia. "I just got so angry when I saw what she'd done. My entire year's work is completely destroyed."

"I understand that, but that is not how we express

our frustrations here." The headmistress sighed, leaning back in her chair. "I'm not sure what to do about this situation. You're still here on probationary status, Lia. This was a very, very poor choice." In the office annex, Lia heard the headmistress's phone ring, and the secretary answered.

"Now, I'm afraid I really have no choice here but to—"

"Ma'am," said the headmistress's assistant, poking her head through the side door, "Ma'am, I really apologize, but there's a call for you."

"Please tell whomever it is that I'll call them back later. I'm busy, Kate."

"She's very insistent, headmistress."

"Who is it?"

"She said her name is Lenore Koroleva."

The headmistress blinked slowly. Lia's eyes widened—what was happening? How had her grandmother already heard about what was going on?

"You can transfer her to me," said the headmistress, and Lia stifled a smile. Her grandmother was the only person she'd ever seen strike a healthy dose of fear into the headmistress. Or maybe it was just respect, but either way, Lia was grateful. Headmistress Chambers picked up the phone on her desk, motioning to Lia to wait.

"Good afternoon, Lenore," she began. "Can I help you?" She listened intently, tapping an ornate pen on the top of the papers stacked on her desk. Lia sat in suspense for over a minute, waiting impatiently to be filled in on what was going on. Finally, the headmistress hung up, folding her hands under her chin again.

"Well?" said Lia. "What did she say? I haven't talked to her recently—we've had some family issues."

"I heard something of the sort," nodded the headmistress. "It wasn't a surprise to me, after your mother's outburst at Parents' Weekend. I scheduled a meeting with you after that event, by the way, and you never responded with your availability."

"I was distracted," muttered Lia. "Sorry about that."

"It's alright," sighed the headmistress. "I should have followed up with you; it just slipped my mind."

Lia wondered how busy the headmistress was. She seemed to have an enormous amount of things going on in her role at the school, but she never looked harried or tired. It was admirable, really. Lia would've cracked under the pressure in her position without a doubt.

"Well, your grandmother has already heard about your incident with Grace. I swear, that woman has more spies than even I know about, and deeper connections than I realized. She'll be here in a few hours to speak on your behalf, so we'll wait for her to arrive."

"What? How? I didn't know she was even in the state."

"She was already on her way to see you, evidently."

"I don't understand. Why wouldn't she tell me?"

Lia reached into her pocket for her phone, which

was turned off while she was in class. Turning it on again, voicemails and messages immediately popped onto the screen. Well, that explained it, then.

"Did she say whether she'd gotten the situation figured out with my mother?"

"She didn't say. We'll have to wait for her to explain exactly what's going on."

Lenore Koroleva was coming to Beverly Hills Prep. Lia felt a warm rush of hope. She'd been so mixed up without her grandmother. Maybe, just maybe, everything would be alright.

Lia waited in the headmistress's office as the day crept by, hour by hour. She was permitted to work on her laptop, but she fidgeted and checked the time obsessively. The reality of the situation she was in was hitting Lia hard. What she'd done had been monumentally stupid. What was going to happen to her? The headmistress was right—she was still technically a probationary student. Her feud with Grace definitely didn't fall into the realm of allowed behavior. Lia gnawed on one of her fingernails and waited.

Finally, the sound of heels tapping briskly on hardwood had Lia leaping out of her chair. The headmistress straightened in her chair as well, though her expression remained as poised as ever. There was a knock at the door, and then Lia's grandmother strode into the room like an empress. She wore an exquisite ice blue pantsuit and heels, and her snowy hair was swept into a severe French knot. Her eyes were the exact same as Lia's and her mother's: a dark, stormy gray, but they softened when she saw Lia.

"Grandmamma!" Lia exclaimed, and then she was in her arms, and the tears she hadn't shed in weeks were flooding out of pure relief. Why did she always cry when she saw Lenore? Maybe because she was the only one who made Lia feel safe, and protected.

"Lia, dear, you stupid little idiot," Lenore said, with her special brand of affection.

"Hello, Lenore," said the headmistress, interjecting

to shake Lenore's hand respectfully. "It's an honor to have you here, as always."

"Pleasure," said Lenore shortly, and the headmistress moved back to her desk.

Lenore held Lia away from her sternly, shaking a finger in her face. "What do you think you're doing, getting into a situation like this? Are you trying to make things more difficult for yourself?"

"I'm sorry," said Lia, and then she explained the situation to her grandmother, telling her how she'd seen her destroyed projects and lost control. Lenore listened intently, pausing to interject with piercing questions. Finally, Lia finished, and her grandmother took the seat next to her, nodding to Lia to indicate she should sit back down.

"Well, this changes everything," said Lenore to the headmistress. "Lia was wrong in getting involved here, but she was clearly provoked by this girl."

"That doesn't excuse the behavior, Lenore."

"Oh, Martha, come now. Let's not be pious."

Lia had to stifle an incredulous smile. *Martha?*

"Punish Lia how you see fit. Suspend her if you like. But expulsion in this case seems extreme."

The headmistress hesitated. "There was another incident with Lia's mother, Lenore. She made an enormous scene at a weekend event."

"I am aware of my daughter's unfortunate behavior at the event."

"I don't know that I can suspend Lia with that sort of parental supervision being her only option as guardian. Her mother clearly doesn't have the capacity to parent Lia in the way she needs, if you'll excuse my saying so."

Lenore nodded coldly, her face darkening as they spoke of Sonia. "My daughter is spoiled to her core, cruel, and selfish. I don't know that I'll ever be able to change that, but I think we can all agree that she is not what's best for Lia. For many years I tried to be a resource for Lia, another person she could depend on, hoping that Sonia would adjust to being a parent given time. But I waited too long. Sonia will never be the parent Lia needs. Lia rebels against everything that Sonia is. The combination is nothing short of disastrous."

"Do you have a suggestion, Lenore?" The headmistress glanced at Lia, and back to her grandmother. "I could try making an exception to the expulsion that Lia should receive if there was some sort of solution we could come to."

"I believe there is. I'm going to become Lia's legal guardian."

Chapter Eighteen

Lia's mouth dropped open in shock.

"Grandmamma, the last I heard was that Mom didn't want you anywhere near me. How did you get her to agree to this?"

"Sonia is not complicated, dear. All she wants is money; that's all it took to get her to drop that ridiculous, groundless restraining order."

"But that doesn't make you my guardian."

"No, it doesn't. We're in the process of changing that, though. As I said, all Sonia wants is money. I offered her a big enough prize, and she traded you for it, as I knew she would." Lenore's voice was matter-of-fact, but dripping with disdain for her daughter's greed.

"Are you serious?" Lia breathed.

"I'm completely serious. I should have done this years ago. I just always hoped that there would come a time when Sonia would grow up, and become a parent. But her priorities will never fall that way, and you were damaged by her in the process. I'm sorry for that, Lia."

"It's not your fault, Grandmamma," murmured Lia. She was in total shock. *How could this be happening?*

"I assume that, legally, the question of Lia's guardianship is still being processed," said the headmistress, and Lenore nodded.

"That's correct. Sonia has verbally agreed, and she's signed off on the paperwork, but the decision isn't final as of yet. A judge will have to approve it."

"I can't believe you already did the paperwork," said Lia. "Why didn't anyone ask me?"

Both Lenore and Headmistress Chambers turned to stare at Lia.

"Is that not what you want, Lia?" her grandmother asked.

"No, Grandmamma, it is. I mean, this makes me really, really happy. But I could've become emancipated from Mom. Then I would've had to support myself, and that would've been fine. I don't want to be a burden on you."

"You are anything but a burden to me," said Lenore. "Don't be foolish."

"Yes, Grandmamma."

The headmistress cleared her throat. "I'm still not sure about this, Lenore. A change of guardianship is a very good start for Lia, in my opinion, but it doesn't change her past behavior. It doesn't change the fact that she violated her probationary guidelines."

"I never said you couldn't punish her," said Lenore. "Punish away. Just don't expel her."

"I don't want to start over again," Lia admitted, glancing up at the headmistress. "I don't really have friends here, but I only have one year left. I'll toe the line, and I'll pass my classes. If I get kicked out of another school, I might never be accepted to college."

Still, the headmistress hesitated, her fingers tapping on the desk. "How can I be sure that Lia will behave for the short time left in this year, and all of her senior year as well? Grace's family won't be happy about the altercation. They'll want some form of punishment."

"What exactly do you want, Martha?"

The headmistress shrugged delicately. "I think starting with a suspension will be a good first step. A full two weeks, and a written apology to Grace."

Lia frowned at that, but her grandmother nudged her shoulder, a signal to keep her mouth shut. "Will that little hoodlum be punished as well? It seems as though she admitted to the willful destruction of Lia's property."

"Grace will be dealt with, yes," said the headmistress smoothly. "But let's focus on Lia. Lia will continue her therapy appointments, and the GPA requirement will stand as well."

"Anything else?"

There was a long pause. Lia thought she saw the headmistress's eyes glitter, sly as a cat.

"The east wing of the grounds needs sprucing up," she said, leaning back in her chair.

Lenore smiled smugly. "I'll write a check," she said.

By the time they were finished in the headmistress's office, the day had disappeared. Lia stretched as her grandmother opened the door for her, rolling her neck. Her body was tense and she felt exhausted.

"Alright, then," said Lenore, briskly efficient. "The security team is already in your room packing you a bag to come home with me. So, all we need to do is leave."

"I can't thank you enough for being here,"

said Lia, "and for doing this for me. I'm sorry, for everything."

"As your guardian, I do expect you to toe the line, Lia. There can be no more of this behavior. I'll give you what you need, but I need your word in return that you'll behave." Her voice was stern, but Lenore's eyes were bright and full of concern. "I want only the best for you, and it will be much easier to make that happen if you put your best foot forward as well."

"I promise, Grandmamma," said Lia. "I really do. I think my therapist has been helpful too. I got mad at him, in our last appointment. I need to apologize."

"You can tell him in two weeks," said Lenore, and she walked Lia to the car with a supportive hand on her shoulder.

Lenore took Lia to one of their favorite places, which was Lenore's redwood mansion deep in the forests of Lake Tahoe, Nevada. The house was Lia's very favorite place to go any time of year, but especially now that it was spring and the creeks were full of crystal-clear snowmelt and the flowers were blooming everywhere. The mansion was three stories, with floor to ceiling windows on one entire side. It was decorated in warm reds and golds, the same colors as Beverly Hills Prep's crest, and the polished staircase wound its way up all three stories.

The first floor housed the steam room and sauna, and a mudroom for changing out of snowy clothes and skis during the winter and swimsuits in the summer. The second floor held the kitchen and dining room, with the vaulted ceilings and the balcony adjacent to the twenty-person polished sugar pine dining table, but Lia's favorite thing was her room on the top floor. It held a queen-size bed with a cozy down comforter and flannel sheets for warmth, and she had her own bathroom with a tub that was practically the size of a pool. Lia had never felt as calm as she did in the days she spent there with Lenore, going on hikes and nature walks and sitting by the fire at night. Lenore was an avid nature photographer, and she kept up with Lia on the most strenuous hikes. She beat her to the top, most days.

At the beginning of the second week of her suspension, Lia started considering an art piece again for the exhibition.

"It seems impossible, Grandmamma," said Lia one morning as they had breakfast. "I don't know how I can make anything good enough to be displayed at this late a date."

She hated Grace for destroying everything, but at the same time, none of those projects had been quite right, anyway. But they were better than nothing, which was now all Lia had.

"You'll come up with something, darling," said Lenore. "I believe in you. The studio is all set up and furnished, so feel free to use it." Lia wracked her brain for ideas.

"Should I paint something? Draw?"

"I prefer your sketches, honestly," said Lenore.

"Which ones?"

"The black ones."

"You like my charcoal work the best?"

Lenore shrugged elegantly as she sipped her tea. "Yes. I like the way you make one medium speak such volumes. Charcoal works should be boring and plain, or at the very least, stark. But yours aren't. I'm not sure how you do it, but your charcoals are your best work. Some artists need color, Lia. You're good enough not to require it."

Lenore nodded to the maid, who took her empty plate to the sink. Lia chewed on her lip, considering her options.

"I could give it a shot," she said thoughtfully.

Lia spent the remainder of the day with a canvas and her charcoal, sitting at the head of one of her favorite streams. She sketched the way the water bubbled and gurgled its way over stones and leaves, the patient way it bore down in its path and inevitably got its way. The trees enveloped her in privacy, and when Lia checked her work she knew it was good. It was the best still life she'd drawn, that was certain.

This was what her other pieces had been missing. This place wasn't just a random location, it was deeply personal to Lia herself, and that was expressed in the drawing. It looked like a drawing of a place she knew, and loved, and that changed the entire composition. But there was another one she wanted to do, and it wasn't a nature feature.

"Grandmamma, will you sit for me?" Lia asked as she returned to the house that night.

"What do you mean, sit for you?"

"For a portrait. Would you sit for me?"

Most women would act modest or embarrassed, but not Lenore. She just nodded and went back to her book. "Of course, dear. We can do it tomorrow morning, when the sunrise comes in over the balcony. I think that will be perfect."

"Me, too," said Lia.

The next morning, Lia sharpened her charcoal stick in preparation for the portrait. She was up early, before the sun, and she shivered in the early morning chill. Lia set up her easel and placed her canvas, angling it just perfectly, and tied her hair up in a high ponytail. Her grandmother came and stood in the place Lia had set up for her just as the sun was rising. Lia angled her face and hands, then stepped back and sat behind her canvas.

"Okay, this is perfect," said Lia. "Just stay exactly like that."

She put her charcoal to canvas, and she started to draw. Lia drew her grandmother's eyes, a shade darker than her own, and she sketched the proud way she held herself and the regal set of her jaw. Her wedding ring was set in white gold, a family heirloom well over two hundred years old, and a priceless treasure that one day would likely belong to Lia. Lia captured Lenore's independence, her fierce spirit, and as she went on, it felt more like a self-portrait to Lia. She saw so much of herself in her grandmother; they had the same cheekbones, the same stubbornness and pride. Lia was tracing the map of her own life as she drew her grandmother's, and the connection tugged at her soul. Drawing her grandmother was like drawing herself, raw and bare, and unapologetically real. She knew at the end of the session, when she blew the excess charcoal off her canvas for the last time, that this was the best work of her life.

"Thank you, Grandmamma," said Lia. "The exhibition is in two weeks. Will you come?"

"I wouldn't miss it, dear. Especially if there's a picture of me on display."

Chapter Nineteen

The day of the design exhibition dawned sunny and clear, and Lia was up with the sun getting ready. Her bedroom was spotless, finally, now that her grandmother had her maids help her unpack when Lia moved back in. The dress she wanted to wear was already laid out, a simple shift of snowy white, with a deep red cardigan. Lia hurriedly showered, then did her makeup and hair with shaking hands. When her curls hung down her back and she'd put on her favorite diamond earrings and necklace, Lia blew out the breath she'd been holding. Her grandmother should be arriving any minute now; she was supposed to go and meet her and then the two of them would attend the exhibition together.

Lia practically sprinted down the hallway toward the Great Hall. Campus was fairly empty, since it was a Saturday. That was fine with Lia—the fight between her and Grace had been the biggest news in school for too long. Lia had written Grace an apology letter and sent it to her, per the headmistress's request, and while she hadn't gotten a response back, she also hadn't had another altercation with Grace. That was enough for Lia. Grace avoided her at all costs now, and the uneasy truce was working just fine. It would suffice until school ended in a few more weeks, at least, and then Lia had heard Grace was considering a semester abroad. It would be a relief to not have to see her for half their senior year.

Dr. Lowenstein had been the only person delighted to see Lia return to campus, not that she'd expected anything less. Their first session after Lia's suspension, they'd gone over time by nearly half an hour. Lia had filled him in on her grandmother's new guardianship, which a judge would be approving officially any day now, and everything in between. Her father had signed off, too, which was just a formality—Lia had known he wouldn't put up a fight. He barely knew his own daughter, anyway. It was easier for him to let someone else handle all the pesky business that accompanied the raising of his child.

"I'm not happy with you getting into trouble, of course," Dr. Lowenstein had said disapprovingly. "But this separation from your parents might be the best thing for you. I underestimated your mother, I admit. I don't know her as well as you do."

"Consider yourself lucky that's true," Lia had muttered.

Now, the day of the exhibition had finally come. Lia's charcoal portrait of her grandmother was on display on the wall in the Great Hall along with paintings and photography samples of every type and size. Lia had matted and framed it herself, and even placed it perfectly for the exhibition. It had turned out beautifully. It was the most personal piece Lia had ever created, and that emotion shone through her work, elevating it to new levels. The hall was already filled with people—students and their families, faculty, administrators, and plenty of official-looking people holding clipboards and peering closely at the art on display. Lia spotted her grandmother near the front doors and waved wildly, working her way through the crowd to meet her.

"Grandmamma! Isn't this amazing!"

"Hello, Lia, dear," said Lenore, never one to skip polite pleasantries. "Yes, it certainly is something."

"Here, my portrait is this way," said Lia. She led Lenore through the crowd to the space where she'd mounted her portrait. It was exquisitely and skillfully done, deceptively simple, and it was clear to any trained eye that this was not amateur work.

"It's lovely, Lia," said Lenore. "Honestly. This is amazing work. We need to celebrate."

"But nothing's even happened yet, Grandmamma. I mean, I didn't win an award or anything."

"That's immaterial. Achievements such as this one

deserve acknowledgement just for their completion. I'm very proud of you, Lia."

"Thank you, Grandmamma," said Lia, beaming. A camera flashed, and behind them, a reporter recognized Lenore and asked excitedly for a photo. Lenore stood proudly with Lia at her side in front of the portrait and allowed her photo to be taken.

"May I ask a few questions, Mrs. Koroleva?"

"If you must."

While she was engaged with the reporter, Lia moved to stand next to her portrait proudly. A tall woman in a gray pantsuit approached, eyeing Lia and her work.

"Did you do the portrait?"

"Yes, I did," said Lia. The woman scrutinized it carefully, coming closer to check the detail of the sketch.

"This is really terrific work. You should be very proud. May I get your name?"

"Of course," Lia stammered. "It's Lia, Lia Koroleva."

"And what year are you?"

"I'm just finishing my third year."

"Lovely," said the woman, noting Lia's name on her clipboard. "I'm with the Rhode Island School of Design; we'll keep an eye out for you next year, assuming you apply."

"Yes, I was planning on it," said Lia, grinning like a loon. "Wow, I'm honored."

Lenore cleared her throat subtly behind Lia, and Lia moved quickly aside.

"Oh, please let me introduce you to my grandmother. This is Lenore Koroleva."

"Very nice to meet you, ma'am. Your granddaughter is very talented. Are you the subject of the portrait?"

"Yes, I certainly am."

"I definitely see the resemblance—to yourself, of course, but also to Lia. It's almost a self-portrait of her. The intricacy of the delicate work she did drawing your hands and eyes especially stands out.

Congratulations, again, Lia. Let me give you my card."

"Thank you," said Lia, thrills of excitement reverberating down her spine. *Is this really happening?*

The Rhode Island School of Design woman moved on and Lia clutched her card like a lifeline as more faculty members came forward to greet Lenore. Lia studied her portrait critically. The woman was right. The sketch was her grandmother, but it was Lia, too, and everything they shared, from bloodlines to the shape of their hands. It was Lia's past and her future all rolled up into one, and for the first time in her life, Lia felt as though she could truly let go of one to focus on the other. There was nothing holding her back anymore—her future was brand new, ready and waiting. All she had to do was be brave enough to put her whole heart into it, and Lia knew, beyond a shadow of a doubt, that was exactly what she was going to do.

THE END